A Ramshackle Home

.ll.

A Ramshackle Home

a novel

FELICIA MIHALI

Translated by **JUDITH WEISZ WOODSWORTH**

Copyedited by Jennifer McMorran
Cover photo: Linda Leith
Cover design: Debbie Geltner
Book design: DiTech

Library and Archives Canada Cataloguing in Publication

Title: A ramshackle home: a novel / Felicia Mihali;
translated by Judith Weisz Woodsworth.
Other titles: Tara brînzei. English
Names: Mihali, Felicia, 1967- author. | Woodsworth, Judith, translator.
Description: Originally published in Romanian. Translated from the French.
Published in French under title: Le pays du fromage.
Identifiers: Canadiana (print) 20230228682 | Canadiana (ebook)
20230228690 | ISBN 9781773901435 (softcover) | ISBN 9781773901442
(EPUB) | ISBN 9781773901459 (PDF)
Subjects: LCGFT: Novels.
Classification: LCC PS8576.I295343 T3713 2023 | DDC C859/.3—dc23

Printed and bound in Canada

Legal deposit - Library and Archives Canada and Bibliothèque et Archives nationales du Québec, 2023

The publisher gratefully acknowledges the support of the Government of Canada through the Canada Council for the Arts and the Canada Book Fund for our book publishing program.

We acknowledge the financial support of the Government of Canada through the National Translation Program for Book Publishing, an initiative of the Action Plan for Official Languages - 2018-2023: Investing in Our Future, for our translation activities.

We are grateful to the Government of Quebec through the Société du développement culturel and the Programme de credit d'impôt pour l'édition de livres—Gestion SODEC.

Linda Leith Publishing
Montreal
www.lindaleith.com

This book is dedicated to my grandmother,
Stana, and my daughter, Adela.

I wish to express my deepest appreciation to
Mathilde Dargnat.

Table of Contents

May

We made the trip from Bucharest to my village without saying a word. Both of us were like deaf mutes. It had become impossible to say anything at all to each other. Despite my stubborn silence, my husband Mihai glanced at me from time to time, to see if I had tears in my eyes. I avoided his gaze by turning my head to the right, pretending to look out the window and watch the countryside flash by. I was not crying, actually. Daniel was busy playing in the back seat, amid the suitcases. Whenever he was bored, he stuck his nose between our seats, leaned up against my shoulder, and watched, as we did, the line of cars ahead of us. Once we got past Rosiori, he asked me if he could have some of the crackers he had spotted in a bag on the dashboard.

The month of May was drawing to a close after a spring that had been warmer than usual. Some of the trees were still in bloom and the wind had dried up the mud on the unpaved roads. In one or two weeks the village would be covered in fine dust. Despite the poor condition of the roads, we managed to reach the last little village, where my parents' old house was located. The big wrought-iron gate was barely hanging on, attached with only two steel wires, just as we had left it five years earlier. The wires came off in our hands as soon as we tried to undo them. The garden was now overgrown with weeds. Before walking in, I looked at the concrete wall surrounding the house. It was decorated with mosaics and had stood up well to the bad weather, apart from the top part where the intricate arabesque design had been worn by the rain. The three of us went in slowly, stepping gingerly along the cement walkway that led from the gate to the house. On either side, the leafless branches of rose bushes protruded like snags, encircling a large expanse of brush. A small gate leading to the chicken coop and the yard around it was attached by an iron hook. As if it had been waiting to be freed for a long time, the gate swung wide open as soon as I unhooked it. My parents' house, on the other hand, seemed surprised to see me again and overwhelmed by our presence. The windows were darkened, shingles on the roof had been torn off by the wind, and paint was peeling from the walls.

I no longer had a key. Where had I put it five years earlier? Perhaps I had thrown it out, but I wasn't sure.

I remembered only one thing about my mother's funeral: on our way back to Bucharest, we had stopped at a little restaurant to get a coffee.

Mihai put my suitcases down on the patio. I had packed haphazardly, throwing in clothes, canned goods, pots, jars of jam, some bedding. Then, without saying anything about the condition of the property, he watched me closely as if he were guessing what decisions I would need to make. I still refused to look at him. Instead, I kept rummaging through the plastic bags that I had filled with some bread and fruit before leaving. Daniel had stopped at the well in the middle of the yard and was looking down into it. He took a stone and threw it in, fascinated by the ripples in the water. A few seconds later, a swarm of wasps emerged from the dark rings of water. Daniel was terrified and began to scream and run toward us. The wasps swirled above our heads and buzzed around the treetops for a while until they finally came to rest in a clump on the branches of the barren pear tree growing next to the large outdoor oven.

Once he saw that I was determined to stay here, Mihai was satisfied that there was nothing more he could do. He said his goodbyes guardedly before leaving us. He didn't ask me to change my mind or go back to Bucharest with him. He was just content to have seen the property that I had inherited from my parents. Yet, the look in his eyes was unmistakeable. The place was in such bad shape that it was discouraging and Mihai was as distraught as I was. But I stubbornly continued to unpack my bags, while Daniel began to explore the garden.

Mihai walked out of the yard quietly and waited in front of the gate for a while before starting the car. For a long time, I listened to the drone of the engine, which summoned me like an insistent prayer. Sitting there on the concrete blocks that bordered the patio, I listened until all traces of the car had vanished and I watched the quivering wasps begin to make their nest in the branches of the sterile pear tree.

My mother had died in a work-related accident five years earlier, two years after the death of my father. It was just after I had met Mihai, the summer when I was finishing up my bachelor's degree in literature. He had been working as an engineer for three years. Not long after we met, we decided we would get married. Although he hadn't known my mother, he took care of the funeral arrangements, together with my old aunts, who knew absolutely nothing about this stranger and who couldn't understand why he was dealing with all those things.

After only three months of mourning, we did get married. There were no frills, we didn't invite anyone, there was no celebration, we told very few people. With the help of Mihai's parents, we bought a small apartment before the onset of winter, in the Rahova neighbourhood of Bucharest. We decorated it very simply with inexpensive furniture, which we picked up here and there in second-hand stores. Our little home, which we continually rearranged and organized during the first year of our marriage, began to look quite acceptable over time, even intimate, with two large wooden cabinets in the dining room, a bookcase we had bought from a Jewish man who was moving to Israel, a saggy couch, two armchairs without arms, a narrow bed in the bedroom, and a small desk we had inherited from my godmother. The floor was carpeted with two mats on which we had placed a wool rug, and the windows were draped with heavy linen curtains.

Daniel was now four years old. He had my genes, and we looked like two peas in a pod. All the time we were together, Mihai had kept the same job. As for me, I had been fired after working for three years as a secretary for an import-export company.

After I was let go, I stayed home for two months. During that time, I sewed two dresses and read a few slim books by great writers. I thumbed through some of the textbooks from my university days, which had been strewn haphazardly on the lower shelves of our bookcase, but I quickly lost interest in them. I knit a woollen throw and became a real burden to my friend Ileana, who had been my classmate.

For two whole months, I revelled in the beautiful spring weather, spending my mornings comfortably seated on the little balcony that overlooked all the other apartment blocks in the neighbourhood, drinking my café au lait in peace. From the time my husband left and my son woke up, I enjoyed a brief but delightful moment of silence. Five years after moving in, I finally had the leisure to watch the morning bustle in the block of houses below, with their roofs and greenery unfolding beyond our building. From the tenth floor, I could observe spring bursting out in little gardens intersected with chicken coops and sidewalks. But, with each new day, and for no apparent reason, I could feel a strange sadness gradually seeping into my soul. For a long time, I wondered about the source of this new mood. I hadn't felt like that when I was fired, or even when my mother had passed away a few years before. Soon after experiencing this odd sensation, I realized what was causing it: the little abandoned house on the streetcorner. Every day, around nine o'clock in the morning, an old man rode up on a rusty bicycle with two bags of groceries hanging from the handlebars. I had been watching him from the very first day, when he began to graft the grapevines and then remove sheets of plastic that had been thrown across a few rows of onions over the winter. There were also three trees on the small plot of land. He painted the tree trunks and pruned the dry lower branches. After a few hours of working around the yard, he would sit down at a small round table, which he had pulled up against the wall of the house. He would take a lunchbox out of his bag and begin to eat.

Not long before I became aware of this inexplicable sadness, I heard the rooster crow for the first time. I had lived in the neighbourhood for five years without realizing that there were any around. The rooster had disturbed me every night when I was a child. Its sharp cry had intruded on my fitful sleep, which was disrupted by dark, liquid dreams, during which I drowned in endless seas of black water. Just before four o'clock in the morning, I would wake up terrified as the cry of the rooster, as shrill as ever, penetrated the wide-open window. Since then, my inner clock has woken me up every morning at dawn, in tune with the outside world.

After he finished eating, the old man would lie down on a lawn chair and fall asleep, his hat pulled down over his face. That was when I stopped watching him, knowing full well that after his nap he would leave again, after carefully locking up the shed where he stored his tools.

While he slept, I gave up looking at him and put my things away. For lunch I would eat French fries and eggs or a bit of meat and drink a large cup of black coffee. Sometimes, I would grudgingly do the dusting and clean the carpet, but I didn't bother with the corners or places where the dirt didn't show. I would cook twice a week. I took after my grandmother and was quite a good cook. Although I didn't have any sophisticated dishes in my repertoire, I could make hearty soups, palatable stews, and an adequate rice pilaf that would still be good, although a bit firmer, after a few days in the fridge. Mihai was not at all fussy. If I wasn't home, he would reheat the food himself, adding a bit of chopped parsley that I'd left in a small glass on the kitchen table.

I would leave the house around eleven o'clock. I would take the 117 bus to Union Square, where I would transfer to another bus to get to Kogalniceanu Square. I would get off at the Izvor Bridge, walk around the giant sculpture of politician and historian Mihail Kogalniceanu, and then go on to Ostasilor, the small street where Ileana lived. She and I had met on the very first day of university and I had been in her thrall ever since. We remained friends even after I graduated. Two years earlier she had had a big fight with her father, a former restaurant chef who had never accepted her lovers. She had left the family home to be with a man who was studying at the theatre school, despite her mother's bitter tears. Since then, she had moved around several times, choosing apartments that were more and more expensive and less and less well situated. At that time, she happened to be living in an area that was almost a slum, located far from the bus stop at the end of a narrow street with dismal lighting. Her apartment was in an old building, and, paradoxically, the rent was exorbitant. The only advantage to this continual upheaval was that each time she moved, Ileana took an object belonging to her landlords, sometimes provoking a terrible scandal. By now, she had amassed an odd, but adequate, dowry made up of a sagging couch, a wardrobe with doors held on by pieces of newspaper, a rug that was ripped down the middle, and a stove on which only one element worked. Although Ileana and her boyfriend didn't work regularly, they were better off financially than we were. She tutored mathematics to several children who were struggling in school, while Ivan, a would-be actor, occasionally got minor parts in German films being shot in the Bucharest subway.

I would arrive unannounced at their place, whenever I felt like it, whether they were eating, making love, or had people over. There was no way around it because, in a moment of weakness, Ileana had given me a key to use in case she was late getting home. On Saturdays and Sundays, I would stay at their place for a long time, while on other days I would only spend a few hours there. I did my best to be home fifteen minutes before my husband got back, just in time to change and feed Daniel quickly. Each time I saw Mihai come in, I cringed in fear of bad news, lest he tell me, "I've found a job for you."

I spent a lot of time with Ileana in her kitchen, which had become a gathering place because of her stove. The rest of the house was close to freezing in winter, but the kitchen remained warm and cozy, despite the heavy odour of fried food that had penetrated all the kitchen walls and cupboards. Throughout the fifty years of communism, people had eaten, drunk coffee, and had discussions in this room. Young people had got engaged, husbands had quarrelled with one another, and children had done their homework. Dissidents had even used the kitchen to draw up subversive little manifestos and sign anonymous letters addressed to top government leaders. I, too, finally had the time to talk to Ileana all I wanted, the two of us comfortably seated around a small table covered with oilcloth, coffee cups lined up next to the salt and pepper shakers and sugar bowl. Behind us, dirty dishes were piled up in the sink, while green beans simmered in a large pot on the stove. I had long discussions with my friend, an unflappable woman with razor-sharp intelligence. For a long time, I was the preferred target of her cynicism. With my past still so present, I could have talked about it constantly, since I was prone to misfortune at any time, always inclined to shed tears over nothing much. I would have liked to tell stories about my grandmother, my grandfather, or my father's sisters to everyone. But each time I tried to share them with Ileana, she would manage to twist my words disdainfully. Filtered by her way of thinking, my memories became painful, unrecognizable, pitiful. Every time that I became impassioned, that I came close to unravelling the mystery of my past, Ivan would make a noisy appearance at the large wooden front door. Ivan Botnovski was born on the other side of the Prut River, in Bessarabia. He was red headed with bangs that hung down to his eyes, covering his forehead. But what had caught Ileana's eye from the beginning was a scar over his upper lip, the right side of which he had torn in an accident. She looked at him amorously, hoping that I would get the message and unburden them of my presence, but I cursed the interloper and all his future progeny. My friend was showering him with excessive attention, but that didn't bother me. I would never leave before five o'clock, no matter what. I was annoying and clingy, but at home I would have been bored to tears. In the afternoon, I found the sight of the little garden that had been so pointlessly cared for by the old man very irritating. In the morning, I liked to watch him work, slowly, with the kind of serenity acquired in old age. After he left, the sight of the empty lawn chair leaning against the chipped wall filled me with as much dread as a dark abyss.

My husband was a person with very few faults. We had married for love, although the love dwindled from day to day. Now I thought that we could have had a little more affection for one another. Mihai was modest and moderate, clean and even elegant, although there was nothing extreme about him. He enjoyed eating copious meals but would never complain if I served him leftover stew several times in a row. He always wanted more, but would nevertheless be content with what life had to offer him. In his thirties he grew a mustache under his Grecian nose. I thought it looked ridiculous, although I didn't say so. I was annoyed by this strip of rough fur that prickled my lips, especially since our love-making sessions were becoming less and less passionate and more and more infrequent. Very often, I had the impression that it was not just our sexual organs but our entire bodies that were rejecting each other. The bed bore unpleasant traces of our nocturnal antics, which were more mechanical than erotic. The warped mattress sometimes gave me a backache; at other times, I felt it in my knees. But the worst thing was when his chin pressed heavily against my collarbone. That made me really nervous. We knew that to make things easier all we had to do was change positions or simply move over to the other end of the bed, but for the sake of convenience we didn't often do it. Daniel's constant presence, too, prevented us from making love during the day, when the indecency of our actions, in the cold light of day, would suddenly transform love into sexuality: the strap of a camisole sliding down over my naked arm, or his underpants dropped down to his knees.

My husband was conscientious enough to avoid being promoted or fired. He went to bed early, after watching the second film broadcast on PRO TV. Before Daniel went to bed, I made a point of telling him out loud that he was to brush his teeth. Mihai knew that this order was also addressed to him, and he was silently irritated. He had never managed to overcome this sole defect in his upbringing, which was almost perfect: he detested toothbrushes. After making a lot of noise flushing the toilet, he would summon the child into the bathroom himself.

When I discovered, purely by accident, that he was cheating on me, my life was upended. I made a very categorical decision quite quickly and without giving it much thought. There was no handwringing and gnashing of teeth. I didn't make a fuss, and I didn't cry. Two months of doing nothing had obliterated my taste for drama.

I just decided to leave the apartment. I was going to take refuge in my parents' ancestral home. Daniel was going to come with me. And Mihai was going to drive us there. Beyond that, I had no idea what I would find there, what I would do there, how long I would stay, and, above all, how I was going to get by in such a desolate place.

My hometown lay somewhere between the small towns of Rosiori and Draganesti-Olt, approximately 160 kilometres from Bucharest. I had left home at the age of fourteen to go to school, and since that time went back only during the holidays or for extremely short visits. I didn't miss the ramshackle houses, the roads that were either dusty or muddy, the smells, or the people. Not one bit. The members of my family were also a burden to me, and they made me nervous every time they came to see me in Bucharest. On the other hand, they had never met Mihai, so they died without knowing what I had become and how my life had developed after a far from promising adolescence.

I had nothing in common with the place to which I was returning now. Above all, I didn't yet think of it as the place where I had originated, where my roots were. Nothing had ever made me miss it or feel nostalgic about it. All this time, I had tried to forget it, to ignore my past, and to distance myself from it with all my heart. I got angry every time I felt trapped in a web of memories, as thin but as strong and robust as a spider's web.

During the two-hour trip from Bucharest to the village, I wondered about the real reason for my return. Mihai had been unfaithful. Wouldn't it have been better if we had had a bit of a fight about it? What if we shouted at one another, what if we spit in the other person's face, what if we pulled each other's hair? My husband was also sorry about the silence into which this misadventure had plunged us. Accidents were inevitable after five years of marriage. That much was obvious. Yet running away, giving in to unhappiness, were extreme solutions. Even dangerous ones.

Whatever Mihai was thinking, he totally understood that if he had tried to stop me from leaving, all hell would have broken loose. He had grasped something fundamental: although I had not actually uttered the word for a very long time, I had made it clear that I wanted to go back "home."

June

I spent a few hours packing my bags before leaving Bucharest. During that time, I combed the entire apartment, looking for things that I felt would be essential. Since getting married, I had never had any personal hobbies or gone on holidays. And now I was really confused. I was not going to the mountains or the seashore, I didn't even know whether I was going to stay in my village for a week, a month, or a year. When my mother was still alive, I was like a guest in my own home. I never cooked, never boiled water, and never made a fire in the stoves. That's why I could not imagine living in a village that was nearly deserted; nor could I picture how the day would unfold from morning to night in such a place. So, I kept my luggage to a minimum.

I took a last look at the bookshelves. Two books caught my eye, Daniel Defoe's *Robinson Crusoe* and Michel Tournier's retelling of his story, *Friday or the Other Island*. While grappling with the greatest sadness I had ever experienced, I was surprised to feel a fleeting sense of joy. A brief shiver ran down my spine from top to bottom. I was ready for the adventure to begin.

As soon as I arrived at my parents' house, I could smell the garden. It was like a fragrant paradise. Half of it was covered in grapevines that were in full bloom. Tendrils, which had not been pruned in five years, crawled along the ground and became so entangled in places that they formed a rambling and impenetrable thicket. The other half of the garden, where my parents used to grow alfalfa in one corner and vegetables in another, was now overgrown with weeds. Some of the most common plants—the most invasive—were thriving: nettles, rhubarb, pigweed, wormwood, rapeseed, quack grass, and skunk cabbage. The fruit trees had sprouted tangled suckers and a little forest of new trees had been seeded from fruit pips scattered by the birds. The trees that I remembered from my childhood were still there, although they were very dry and twisted: two apple trees, two pear trees, a plum tree, and a cherry tree. The lane that ran from the outer gate to the front door of the house was lined on either side with petunias and hardy perennials with sticky, bittersweet sepals. These rebellious plants had finally escaped the tyranny of my mother. Every spring, she would attack all the native plants that grew on their own and replace them with all kinds of flowers—unscented ones with brightly coloured petals, which were waxy looking as if they were made of plastic. During the scorching summers, she took care of these pretentious plants, which sprang from bulbs as swollen as herniated testicles.

The king of the garden, the rose bush, had been my mother's favourite by far. Their obvious love affair made them the envy of everyone. Mother, so proud of the virility of the vegetal male, had planted it right next to the stone wall. But when its small roots, contained in an inverted flowerpot, reached maturity, its thorny branches completely invaded the laneway. In the spring, the prickles covering the stems looked like the tiny claws of newly hatched chicks. But in the fall, when the rose bush was about to rebloom, when the green sepals were fighting with all their might against the explosion of red petals, they would turn into veritable eagle talons. They would lie in wait for a chance to snag your clothing or scratch your skin. In the fall, after the whole garden had been devastated, ravaged by the summer sun, my mother's rose bush, still green, dominated the empire of pale grasses. The other flowers had long since scattered their seeds across the ground, to no avail, while the rose bush remained in heat and excited the air as it excreted its pheromones.

Unfortunately, after my mother died, the rose bush also became stunted. Nettles and common pigweed had wound themselves around its branches, down to the testicular bulb, squeezing the hairy scrotum. Out of loyalty to its beloved, my deceased mother, it haughtily resisted the indecent advances of these vegetal courtesans.

I didn't worry about the warfare among the plants. Once I had set foot on the scene of my childhood, I just carved a narrow path through the weeds up to the middle of the garden, where I set up a table and a chair under one of the two apple trees. Daniel felt at home in this semi-wild bush. He felt like an explorer in Africa. The first childhood secret I shared with him was capturing a little earth monster we called "The Old Ball," an ugly creature that lived in the dry ground and looked like a giant spider. The only way we could make it come to the surface was to flood its hole with water. I made a net for Daniel to use for catching butterflies or trapping the moths that were defoliating the trees by depositing their larvae on the branches. It only took him a few days to become an expert in moles, too, chasing them all the way to their burrows and disturbing their habitat.

His calves were raw, with trickles of blood that made his leg look like a map on which you could read the history of his days and the route he took on his expeditions. His fingers were covered in blisters, which hurt a lot when he took his bath in the evening. His little face was sunburned, puffed up like a bun, and his lips were coated with a thick, whitish crust, with cracks which sometimes oozed with blood. His hair was in disarray and dry snot would collect at the base of his tiny nose. His ears, blocked by a build-up of ear wax, poked through the mess of hair, dust, and blades of grass.

I no longer kept a close watch over him. We hardly spoke to one another. At mealtime, I would spread two pieces of bread with pâté or soft cheese, put them on a plate, and leave the plate on the table outside. When he found them, they would be dried out or sometimes infested with ants. Famished, he would brush the ants off and devour the bread all at once, all the while running after butterflies or holding a little mole in one hand.

The first week, I read the little book by Tournier. I would postpone reading the end of the book, which I had been familiar with for a long time, and which no longer meant anything to me, like many other things, actually. When I finally got to the last page, I went back to the beginning, which was the only part of the book that seemed to shed some light on my own existence. On board a ship that was going to wreck on the shores on an unknown island, in the middle of a storm, Captain Van Deyssel placed a deck of tarot cards on a table in front of Robinson and told him that everyone had his own way of structuring the world around him.

Barely one month had gone by and I already had proof that I was lazy.

Was I unhappy? I kept quiet about it. The time that I wasted, moaning, lying on my bed, analyzing for the thousandth time what had happened between me and my husband was no longer important. Finally, I had come around to believing that it was just an accident. Why the strange coincidence, watching the old man quietly tending his garden at the very same time as I was finding love letters my husband had received from a certain secretary? My despair seemed to echo what my grandfather used to call "the time for tears," those few days in spring when the freshly trimmed dry grapevines would shed a few salty tears after a few strokes of the pruning shears. The two events were not isolated, independent of one another; they could not be separated. My sadness, truth be told, was perhaps not even authentic. I was suffering, but at the same time I was certain that everything that had happened could not have happened in a different way.

During the first month, Daniel and I nearly died of hunger. We were also becoming infected with lice. And fleas, too! One evening, a little dog wandered into our yard. We adopted him immediately and he had been sleeping with us ever since. During the day, he would roam the countryside looking for his mother, but when nightfall came, he would reappear, under our bed, bringing us more and more new parasites.

I had thrown all kinds of useless things into our suitcases, including toiletries we would never use because we didn't have a bathroom. I had brought dishes without realizing that we didn't have the wherewithal to keep a fire going for more than fifteen minutes. I would have paid a lot of money to buy a simple gas camping stove, because I didn't know how to use the old rural methods, that is to burn dried sunflower stalks or, even worse, wheat straw.

Beyond the henhouse and the little yard around it, there was a fence that enclosed what was left of the old outbuildings: a pigsty without a roof, a pen for the goats with only two walls still left standing, and a haystack that was pretty much rotten. At the back of the property lay a large pile of sunflower stalks that looked as if they would disintegrate if touched. Everything, in fact, looked like it was decomposing, gradually turning into earth, trying to dissolve and blend into the dust.

Inside the house, the kitchen hearth remained intact. On the brick floor stood a tripod above which hung a blackened chain that once held a large cauldron used to cook polenta. On the other side of the fireplace was the little door of an oven used only in winter to bake bread. Inside I saw the pans on which my grandmother used to bake her onion, parsley, and cheese pies. China cabinets lined the walls on both sides of the room. In the basement, I found large bins which had been used to store flour and salt pork, as well as three wine barrels, whose wood was still imbued with acids from the fermenting process.

In order to put all of this to good use eventually, I would have to do some housework first. I would have to waste days on end washing up and putting things away. But I felt incapable of the slightest effort. I was content to feed Daniel bread and pâté and to wash him when mud began to peel off his feet like the bark of a tree. We washed our clothes in cold water, but not until they had become rough and scratchy.

For an entire month, then, I contemplated the ruins around me. I wandered from morning till night, from one end of the dying village to the other. You could spend entire days without running into a living soul. In the odd place, you could see footprints or pawprints left by dogs. The ditches were filled with ground ivy. None of the houses had gutters to drain their wastewater. Fences had disappeared so that if you stood in the street, you could see right into the middle of the yards, where little houses stood. Sometimes, there was not much more than a dilapidated wooden frame left. I rarely saw curtains on the windows. The only living creatures that crossed my path were scruffy little cats, who seemed to intrude on the deathly silence of the place by climbing up to the tops of the fenceposts, or an occasional dog running across the narrow road without paying much attention to me.

Only one house out of ten in the entire village was inhabited. Sometimes, I happened to be greeted by an old lady with a fossilized face and a black scarf wrapped around her neck and chin, sitting out on the front steps of her tumbledown home. I would just nod at women like this, making a soundless greeting that would elicit the same response from them. Only once did one of them ask me who I was and who my parents were. I told them my name, but the old lady didn't remember anything. When I talked about my grandmother, she could scarcely place the family. She lowered her scarf slightly to uncover her dried lips and spoke to me about what I was like when I was little, about how everyone was surprised that I had such a little mouth, a tiny one that was no bigger than a dot, as the women of the village would say to my mother, who for some reason was proud of my mouth as if it were a thing of beauty.

There was a bit more life in the centre of the village. The post office was still in operation, as was the telephone exchange. There was even a general store about three kilometres from my house. There was still a municipal office, but there was no longer a medical clinic, a barbershop, or a bakery. Bread was brought in every Monday from the nearest town. On the other hand, two taverns remained, each patronized by its five regulars.

The shelves in the store were filled with everything countryfolk needed, ranging from basic bread to rubber boots, including pasta, tomato juice, lye, heating oil, matches, salt, thread, underwear, pickaxes, nails, aluminum spoons, buckets, cuckoo-clocks, slippers, and combs. Some items, like a modest little pencil or something resembling a notebook, were nowhere to be found, as if they had been banned. You couldn't find a toothbrush, toothpaste, cotton balls, window screens, rat poison, or mosquito repellant.

At this end of the village, at around four o'clock in the afternoon, you got a chance to see people who were a little younger and maybe a few children. I don't know whether there were any more than ten of them in the entire village. The church was still standing, but Sunday mass had not been celebrated for a long time. The large sculpted wooden door was open on the occasion of funerals only. The priest, one of my many cousins, had been living in another village since his second marriage, which was outlawed by the Orthodox Church. Each time the villagers required his services, they would call him reluctantly and out of pure necessity, with the assistance of a third party. Because of his forced exile, my cousin would recite the mass grudgingly, leaving out big chunks of the Scriptures. My mother told me that one time, during the national football championships, he had stopped a funeral procession in its tracks to go into a small house and find out what the score was.

The school had long since been shut down. My old teachers were dead or had moved away. The younger teachers commuted to different villages where there were still enough children to teach. In winter and in summer, they made these trips by bicycle. Once a week, a doctor would come to the dispensary, which was now down to one room, to give injections to sick people or to write out prescriptions for the most common ailments in the area: diarrhea, the flu, hemorrhoids, ulcers, trichinosis from eating pork, constipation, or bronchitis. The grocer was authorized to fill these prescriptions and had even begun to give advice to patients who flocked to his gloomy little shop in desperation.

I didn't know which of my close relatives were still alive. My mother's brothers had moved to Rosiori a few years earlier and, of my father's four sisters, only the youngest was still alive and she probably didn't know that I had come to the village. Around our house, everything seemed deserted and derelict. My only neighbours were two widows. One lived behind us while the other lived three houses away.

My godmother, my grandfather's sister, had lived on the edge of our property. You could still see the run-down stable and the side wall of her house, on which the damaged plaster looked like a slightly truncated map of Australia. Behind it was a summer kitchen, with a crumbling fireplace, where my cousin Manole, who was three years older than me, used to press wild plants for my herbarium using an old coal-fired iron. I could still remember how stems oozing with sap would sizzle as they were instantly flattened by the iron before being glued on to sheets of kraft paper.

Until I was ten years old, my family had forbidden me to speak to Manole because our grandmothers had quarrelled when they were young. It was with this cousin that I had tried to make love for the first time, at the age of thirteen, in the shade of a plum tree at the back of his parents' garden. We got inside a burlap sack, lay down on the ground, and that was all.

On rainy days, Manole and I would stay on the patio, both of us leaning against the wooden railing, watching the raindrops trickle down. His grandfather would be shelling the maize and we, the children, would carry the kernels to the upper attic.

Every abandoned house had its own story, sometimes more than one. Each of them stirred up feelings in me, but they were fleeting memories that didn't make me very happy. I always said that I didn't have a pleasant past. I was always loath to acknowledge my origins. And, above all, I never spoke openly about my childhood or my parents.

There was nothing to tell. I always passed over this chapter of my life as quickly as possible. On all the administrative forms or papers that I had to fill out, I wrote these dates quickly, feeling almost ashamed of my personal history. I felt no gratitude toward my ancestors, and I was not the only one who felt this way. We all had a big complex about our roots. The past was a heavy burden for all of us. It was there, in our souls, but it brought no joy. Everything that awakened a memory of the past, everything that was closely related to it, felt like an unpleasant weight on our shoulders.

During my pilgrimage through the village, there was only one house that I wrenched from the silence and oblivion into which it had fallen. It was the house opposite ours, on the other side of the street, which had been inhabited by a shepherd, the most violent man I have ever met. The property had been abandoned for seven years, that is, it had already been deserted before my father died. The roof had been almost completely torn off by the wind, the concrete slab fencing had collapsed and begun to crumble piece by piece, blending in with the weeds and the soil. Bold briars had crept up to the windows, climbing over the cracked windowpanes. Their leaves cast indiscreet glances at the rooms inside. The carved wooden door, the most beautiful one in the village—where everything was otherwise ephemeral, humble, and shabby—still stood proudly, resisting decay. Green paint, the green so common on all the wood-frame houses in the village, was peeling off like paper. This was the house where I had so often eaten borscht. The shepherd's two daughters had hung a swing from the branch of a quince tree. I had whiled away most of the days of my youth there, to my mother's chagrin. When our parents were looking for us, we would hide in the hayloft that had been built above the sheep pen.

I forced the door of the house open. It was not locked but the iron hinges had rusted and grown stiff. It was a perfect example of houses in the region, the Boianu Plain. In the front there was a small vestibule with doors leading to two rooms: on the left was the living room, where the whole family used to gather, in the daytime and in the evening, in summer as well as winter; on the right was a guest room, that would have been decorated with drapes and carpets, but also used as storage space. There would have been a jumble of stuff stashed there, in trunks or on a coat rack—clothes for holidays and funerals, dowry items, bags of wool, old children's clothing that would be handed down to younger siblings. There would be no furniture in the vestibule, other than a small table for the water bucket. From there, the kitchen door opened onto a long, narrow room the size of the other two combined.

The house was completely empty, with the exception of some nails still lodged in the walls and in corners near the mouseholes. This nudity was to become my nightmare. During the suffocating nights of summer, when sleep eluded me, I felt imprisoned. Terrified, I awaited the apparition of Aunt Ilinka's face, burned by fire, full of sores, the way she looked when I saw her for the last time before she died. The woman was coming closer and reaching out to me with pus oozing from the blisters that covered her hands. She had burned herself by blowing out an oil lamp. The entire village had paraded through her yard to see her swollen face as it blackened. I had grown up with her two daughters; they had been my closest friends throughout my childhood. Back then, I had felt contempt for them because they were shepherd's daughters, but in their company, I had always had the most exquisite sense of freedom. Their presence did not make me feel uncomfortable and I was able to look them directly in the eye. The bond between us derived mainly from the crude things we used to do together. We discovered the secrets of our bodies, without too much trouble and a little earlier than other youngsters. It wasn't clean and it wasn't elegant. But these intimate actions made us more mature than people usually are at that age. In the fall, when the leaves began to fall, the three of us slept out on the patio, covered in a large sheepskin. I waited as long as I could before falling asleep so that I could watch the other two girls doze off. I was barely twelve years old and I was already feeling tired. Looking at their serene faces, listening to their heavy breathing, I got a glimpse of how oppressive the future would be.

I had had so many neighbours. How had they lived and how had they died? There had been so many stories and they weighed on me.

That which had disappeared was completely dead and wasn't worth talking about. That which no longer existed was no longer important. Did I really need to remember? If the tragedy of these people was useless and inconsequential, why bother talking about it? It should be forever forgotten.

But despite my stubborn refusal to remember, it took me only a few weeks to realize that this world did have a certain importance. I had once belonged to it and saw myself reflected in many of its elements. And no matter what I wished for, I could no longer completely obliterate the past. I belonged to it more that I was willing to admit.

It didn't take me long to recover from the breakdown of my sense of smell. For me, after all, smell had been prime. I was blind, deaf, and mute. But I have always known how to smell, even sniff out, the world. Everything around me would become quickly engraved on my brain just by following the two dark channels of my little nose. If I had to find someone, someone like me for example, I would do it exclusively by means of my sense of smell.

A simple aroma, the slightest whiff, a light fragrance—imperceptible scents for most people—would kindle my spirit. Certain perfumes would make me happy, while others would fill my soul with despair. I could love or hate a person just by having sniffed the scent of their skin or the type of cologne they used. Certain kinds of smells would make my stomach churn: sheep's cheese, rancid butter, gasoline, bleach, wet sheep's wool, the skin of goats when they come into heat in the fall, some men's perfumes, an unclean penis. I liked only light odours, indefinable ones: flowers on trees or vines, corn silk, ripe quince, Daniel's skin when he was little, hair that hadn't been washed for two days, sour soup. Each season had its own distinctive aroma: in the fall, the smoke of burning leaves; in winter, pork stewed with wild celery; in the spring, the fragrance of sweet violets blooming in the graveyards; in summer, the mud along the riverbanks where tadpoles remained trapped after a drought.

In the city, I used to spend a lot of time wandering past the flower market, fishmonger, or smoked sausage stand. Food that smelled delicious would whet my appetite. I just needed to smell something to feel it titillating my tastebuds. Flat bread, red wine with a lot of tannin, fried fish, canary melons, ripe pears, raisins, caramel, cooked squash and beets, halva, corn on the cob, onion pie, sesame snaps, green tomato salad, sauerkraut, syrupy pastries. I liked heavy, saturated tastes that summoned all parts of the tongue at the same time, a morsel of food that was at once sweet, salty, sour, peppery, and fragrant.

On the other hand, I found the stench of the city disgusting; it made me want to vomit. My first experience in the city was clouded by the odour of bleach, which I had never smelled before going to the lycée. The first time I went into the dormitory toilets, the toxic fumes made me ill. There was a sticky, white residue of cleaning agent on the floor. I felt a burning sensation deep in my nose and I began to sneeze until tears welled up in my eyes. I couldn't get over it. I was afflicted with constipation for a long time. Even at the time, the effects were devastating. Some girls had dipped their fingers in excrement or menstrual blood and scribbled graffiti on the cream-coloured walls of the bathroom stalls. One summer, the tutor who supervised us even checked our panties. Those who had their period were forced to clean the soiled walls.

Waking up in the morning in the huge dormitories and breathing in the fumes of bleach felt like a nightmare. The immaculate, well laundered bedsheets, which still retained the odour of that damn substance, didn't give me the chance to forget the white sediment on the toilet floors, even at night. One of the maids would mop the great hall, briskly swabbing the stone floors and energetically wiping down the side walls. The room was filled with the sounds of dormitory doors squealing and plastic slippers scuffing. The girls filed into the large bathroom with its broken sinks, some without taps, rushing to get their morning ablutions over with. The same endless line-ups at the few sinks that were not yet clogged up and still worked could be seen through the open windows of the building just across the way, where the boys lived.

I would wait as long as I could to get up. During this time, my nose would analyze the odours of the bedding with the precision of a detective. After eliminating the smell of bleach, I discovered other ones I was equally familiar with. I buried my nose in the sheets and, one by one, lightbulbs lit up on the sensitive map of my brain: piss and dirty genitals on my pyjamas, which I never changed often enough, oily hair, the acrid smell of armpits. Deep down, I detected the smell of the woollen blankets that were never aired out, and of the mould, rust and sawdust of the mattress and springs. Bits of jute from the carpet, which had been sprayed with water, were strewn everywhere and the broom used to remove dust bunnies and cobwebs was lying around. Cheap toiletries of the Communist era had their particular scent: Cristal toothpaste spread on a wet toothbrush, Mirage deodorant spray, and Clef soap. Voices and sounds, on the other hand, didn't get on my nerves nearly as much. I was less bothered by the laughing, shouting, and crashing of books on the floor, by the rustling of the pages of a notebook, by the squeaking of doors, or by the clicking of heels on the tiled floor, all of which reminded me of nothing more than the laborious daily trek to our school, a lycée in the Camp Road neighbourhood.

The dining hall, where we ate three times a day, was another place full of surprises in my daily routine. Soiled tablecloths, metallic-tasting jugs made of pitted enamel, greasy dishes, overly sweet tea, accompanied by a chunk of black bread, a small cube of margarine and a spoonful of marmalade. From the open door of the kitchen, the smell of boiled vegetables, cooked meat, and thick gravy hovered over the dining room. I also noticed details that escaped the others girls: the immense cauldron of boiling water in which all the dishes were being washed without detergent, the open sewer under the sink, the larder with bins of sprouted potatoes that attracted bugs, half frozen and rotten red onions, preserves and canned peas covered with a layer of dust, bottles of oil with rusty caps, packets of weevil-infected pasta, smoked bacon hanging on a string from the ceiling, dried herbs in cheesecloth bags, sacks of salt and macaroni, aluminum milk cans, pails of yogurt.

Outside, the stench of gas fumes covered everything. You could no longer make out the smell of the trees, the grass, women's perfume, tobacco, and the flower and fruit stands. They were just an optical illusion.

In the afternoon, the girls were forced to do their homework in the study hall for four hours. There, they would doze off with their heads on their desks, letting subdued odours float around the room, carefully camouflaged ones like the occasional discreet fart, tainted with the scent of onion or garlic, a sweaty armpit sprayed with cologne, or hair speckled with dandruff that was tied up in a bun.

At university, I learned how to smell the cold. The amphitheatres and seminar rooms tucked away under the roof, as well as the library, all reeked of the cold, each in its own distinctive way. The washrooms were a bit cleaner than at the lycée. University students were less interested in using finger painting to express their creativity. Gross things were now written out with coloured markers. Pools of urine on the floor were like mirrors in which one could gaze at one's genitals and admire their finest details. The door had a well-placed opening that allowed little voyeurs to photograph the girls' private parts. The big assembly halls, more welcoming than the classrooms, had radiators tucked under the wood panelling.

The odours of my childhood and adolescence had shaped my entire life. Apart from those ones, I had not acquired many others, except for the smell of blood when my son was born.

The world of the village was rather poor in colours and sounds. The seasons were almost monochromatic. It was a kingdom of complementary shades, unsaturated half-tones: pale green, straw yellow, stone grey, reddish orange, milky white, laundry blue. Images did not appeal to my myopic eyes. Later, I was even less sensitive to the visual. I could not judge colours, which for me did not hold the magic power to stimulate or disrupt my memory the way smells did.

Similarly, music did not move me or stir anything up in my soul. Sounds landed in my ears as if they were falling into a bottomless pit. I even forgot who had composed some of the most famous tunes. Only once did I take the time to listen to music. It was during the holidays. I had bought a recording of Weber's music and I listened to it until I wore the record out.

As for my sense of touch? Everything here was covered in dust. You couldn't touch anything without feeling fine sand biting the delicate folds of your skin. The frames of the houses were lumpy, scaley, rarely painted. The steel was hard, cold, rusty. Winter humidity intensified the feel of wet woollens and dog hair. Springtime brought mud that would stick to your shoes and leave dirt on your pants all the way up to the knees.

Like a bird, I would have been able to find my way just by following familiar scents. There wasn't just one, but rather hundreds of odours that blended into a single, strange one that had a dangerous, hostile, and nasty name from which I feverishly tried to distance myself, a name that I still refused to utter.

With so many shortcomings, how would I ever manage to become a normal and complete person? I felt like one of those hybrids conceived in a test tube, lacking the essential elements to be called a human being. I was blind, deaf and mute, and that was no doubt the secret reason for all my failures. But I had never suspected that it could be so serious.

If I had accepted the smell of cheese, from the beginning, my entire life might have changed.

July

In July, once the hot weather started, our lives became easier, even happy. First of all, because I no longer had to worry about Daniel's personal hygiene and laundry. First thing in the morning, I filled a large copper tub with water and placed it in the middle of the yard in full sun so that by evening the water would reach a temperature of around twenty degrees, which was quite acceptable for a bath. I washed Daniel in a little bathtub before sundown and then watched him to make sure he wouldn't get dirty again. He had had a cold for an entire month because we had been using cold water. The well we had in the yard had been dry for a long time, so I had to carry water in two buckets from the big well in the village square. All day I did my best to conserve every drop of water. I washed our clothes the same way, with water heated by sunshine. But we didn't get very dirty. We kept our clothing to a minimum, wearing only a few T-shirts, one pair of pants and a sweater. On days when it was very hot, Daniel wore only a pair of short pants, and I would put on a simple black tank top that came half-way down my thighs.

We used almost no dishes. For two months I had made a few cups of tea using an electric immersion heater. The rest of the time, we would eat bread on which we spread pâté, marmalade, and canned meat. Now we finally had fruit. The trees of the deserted neighbourhood yards had produced ripe apples and red and sour cherries. I would wander through the abandoned fields, returning with a basket full of fruit. We would eat them mainly with bread. However, Daniel would get terrible diarrhea after that kind of meal, so I decided to stew the fruit instead. After that, we ate nothing but compote for all three meals.

In July, I also began to take care of the house a bit more. When we arrived, we had settled into my grandparents' house, which was smaller and much more convenient. After the old folks had died, my parents had moved in, abandoning their vast house for good, turning it over to the mice and insects. The smaller house was basically a shack, which had only one main room, with a large, ceramic-tile stove, and a small kitchen equipped with a chimney and brick fireplace. On one side of the room was the door to the cellar, which you reached by going down two stone steps. When I was a child, the house had a narrow open patio on top of a root cellar where grains of wheat and kernels of corn were stored.

The large house that my parents had built when I was five years old was located a few steps away from the smaller one. It had four rooms, a vestibule, and a glassed-in veranda. However, my mother had used only two rooms all her life. Later, a small bathroom was built between the two buildings. The outbuildings were located in the other yard, separated by a chain link fence. The lay-out of the ancient property had not changed a bit during my five-year absence. I had grown up here with my entire family, each of the couples living in their own house. After I left to go to the lycée, my parents moved into the little bathroom that separated the two houses and which no longer served its original purpose.

During the harsh winters, they heated the house with an electric radiator. My grandmother used to scold my mother for this because she preferred her blue-tiled wood stove, next to which she would spend the long, grey days of winter. But each woman always found something to hold against the other.

After my grandparents passed away, my mother felt liberated. She could finally indulge in her penchant for organization and construction, as the daughter of a mason, the only one in the village. My father would continually grumble, although he never really got involved. He didn't object to anything, but he didn't lend a hand either. Happy with the work he did, he would leave home at dawn and return in the evening, sometimes very late, and very drunk, so tired that he would try to avoid the fights that his wife would want to pick with him.

My mother took over the little house after my grandparents died. The rooms in the larger house had been locked up and then forgotten. The front patio had been glassed in and renamed a veranda. My mother had had a sloping extension added to the roof, so that the old folks' main room became completely shaded. There was never any sunshine in the room. You couldn't tell whether it was morning, noon or night, whether it was nice out or whether it was raining. The kitchen had been renovated and turned into a bedroom in the summer. A dark corner of the veranda was used for cooking although, subsequently, when my mother realized that it was neither good looking nor economical, she began to cook outdoors. In the years that followed, my mother had another shed built, which served as a place to store all the worn-out clothes and rags that were cluttering up our bedrooms. She also put in a gas burner and then brought over the old cabinet and carved wooden shelves where dishes had been displayed and left to collect dust and flies. Torn clothes, burlap sacks, a moth-eaten sheepskin coat, woollen socks with holes in the heels, and faded carpets were piled on top of a large wooden barrel, used to make sauerkraut in winter. A small oven, barely big enough to bake a few baguettes, stood against the outer wall of the shed. Mother had given up on the large outdoor oven in the middle of the yard, where my grandmother used to bake bread for an entire week.

But things did not stop there. Next to the little oven, my mother had commissioned the construction of another shed. At the beginning, no one had a clue what it would end up being used for, not even the commander-in-chief who was waging war on her surroundings. To start with, once the plastering was finished, my mother moved everything she had found in the inside basement: the bins of flour and salt pork and the three wine barrels. To do so, she had to walk through the veranda and the old kitchen each time. Although this made it tidier, it did not stay that way for long. During the summer, rags were also stored in there. The disarray of the outdoor kitchen spread to this latest building, the last in the chain of unnecessary constructions. The family sometimes used it to stash buckets of food for the pigs, sacks of wheat to be milled, or bags of flour that needed to be emptied into the bins in the cellar. In the fall, they put beets, watermelons, and potatoes in there to protect them from the frost. My mother had not foreseen that the building would be built over the chicken coop, preventing the chickens from getting in. Surprised by the project, the hens gave up their comfortable cottage and went to spend their nights perched on the wooden beam hanging over the small oven between the two outbuildings. One winter, which was harsher than usual, there were even goats housed in the latest shed, but the foul-smelling pig was never allowed to sleep that close to the house.

Inside the house, every patch of floor and every piece of furniture was covered in hand-embroidered fabric of all kinds, with cotton sometimes laid over the woollens. Mother had a sense of cleanliness and tidiness, but in reverse. She had given up everything associated with convenience, hygiene, pleasure, or intimacy in exchange for the appearance of elegance. In winter, she wouldn't light the fire until it was very late so she wouldn't have to stir up the ashes. Whether it was windy, raining, or snowing, she would do the washing and cooking outside to prevent the house from getting damp and smelling like food. Also, she had decorated or whitewashed even the things that you wouldn't usually paint over: wood panelling, bricks, and steel. She had a primitive, carnivalesque style for everything. The big windows of the veranda were now brightly coloured, embellished with nylon curtains. The cement floor was covered with linoleum on top of which lay large pieces of fabric. Sheer draperies had been hung from the frames of inside doorways, although this did nothing to keep out the mosquitoes. The ancient icons depicting the apostles had disappeared from the house along with the beautifully embroidered tapestries in two colours, red and black, which had once decorated the walls of our ancestors. Instead, there were now multicoloured cotton wall hangings decorated with roses, cuckoos, and triangular arabesque motifs intertwined with vines and grapes, along with paintings of red or yellow watermelons lying next to a vase or a bowl of apples or pears. I couldn't begin to count the number of curtains with which the windows were festooned, each one more colourful and ornate than the next.

My parents were of the post-1940s generation. It was the generation of nylon, stretchy underwear, pinkish and greenish hues, ready-made clothing, skirts of all lengths, Chinese slippers, Russian overalls, quilted jackets, head-scarves imported from Syria that were decorated with silver thread, copper mugs and plates, gaudy murals with large, sparkly pink flowers and others depicting *The Abduction from the Seraglio*, and carpets made in Iran or Iraq where our workers went to drill for oil.

Personally, I felt an affinity for those that preceded my parents' generation: the former aristocrats of the village, the religious royalists, born during or after the Great War, who used to sleep in long cotton nightshirts stitched with red and black thread. My grandfather wore gumboots, which had replaced *opinca* footware, the donkey or pig-skin sandals once worn by peasants. You always knew when he was nearby by the sloshing sound his shoes made. He always wore a belt made of red wool, even in summer. Until the end of his life, he carried a small well-sharpened knife, with which he cut bread or carved fruit into little pieces. His white linen shirts, with sleeves gathered at the shoulders, were sewn by my grandmother, who spent three days working on each one of them. Both my grandparents were clean, even though they only bathed once a week. Their sweat was not unpleasant, it didn't stink. They perspired like the saints. Their bodies retained their own energy. I believe that the sour smell of sweat originated with collective farming, with the transport of workers in open trucks to their place of work where their faces were covered with dust, with women who wore trousers under their skirts and fur hats under their scarves, and with men who wore stretchy socks inside fake leather boots, who sported Russian caps with ear flaps, and who drank themselves to death on cheap alcohol spiked with ethanol.

What distinguished my grandmother from my mother was her sense of property. While the old lady religiously hung on to each swatch of fabric and meticulously looked after her belongings, my mother neglected everything. She didn't mend or patch anything, she didn't alter clothing or sew buttons back on. My grandmother, on the other hand, would refurbish old clothes and turn them into attractive pieces of clothing. She would not simply add a piece of cloth indiscriminately; she would never patch even old rags without carefully choosing the colour, and her mending was always invisible. Clothes were perfectly folded in her dresser and stored so they wouldn't have wrinkles. Underneath those clothes, she would hide her money, in perfectly flat bills. Although everyone knew about the hiding place, no one laid a hand on her money. For my grandmother everything had its own place in the house, while my mother never could find what she was looking for. She would begin a thousand tasks at the same time without completing any of them, leaving the house to go visiting for hours on end, which would exasperate her mother-in-law. She had nothing to hide, nothing to protect, and nothing to care for.

My grandparents were thin and very tall. They had long faces with sharp features, hieratic features like those of Byzantine saints. They were familiar with the Bible and a lot of things passed down in folklore about the Apocalypse and the life of Jesus. They often repeated the Ten Commandments. The illnesses they suffered from were of their own choosing: my grandmother bore her diabetes with dignity and my grandfather did the same for his stomach ulcer. My parents were obese and soon became flabby, with puffy purple bags under their eyes and revoltingly bad breath. Women of their generation were plagued with vaginal discharge; afflicted with rheumatism, they would suffer from swelling or bowing of the legs when they walked. Men grappled with hemorrhoids, hernias, arthritis, and sometimes tuberculosis. Their hair was full of dandruff. My parents had lost the habit of cutting their nails, which chipped off and grew sharp on their own. With the first days of spring, the skin on their cheeks turned into a kind of dry, waxy parchment. They almost never went to church, they prayed to God only twice a year, at Christmas and at Easter. Celebrating mass terrified them.

During the month of July, then, I began to tidy up my grandparents' shack, which my mother had made unrecognizable. To begin with, I stripped the walls and floor. Now, you could walk in and keep your shoes on all the way to the bedroom. I removed all the fussy frills from the windows and scrubbed the windowpanes, which were covered in bugs. I replaced the heavy woollen bedspreads with light ones made of linen or hemp fibre, which my mother had always avoided because she considered them too plain. Then I put all the kitchen cabinets back in their original place and removed all the old rags that had been stored inside.

The changes were visible. They aroused a sense of euphoria in me and gave me an appetite for work. I loved the almost vacant and natural atmosphere of the room. Building on that feeling of accomplishment, I took on the yard. But this time around it was not so easy. The first thing that caught my attention was the tall bread oven standing near the well. It was rundown, an eyesore, but I didn't know how to get rid of it. I was going around in circles, unable to figure out how to tear it down. The clay walls had crumbled inside and there were only a few tiles left on the roof. But dealing with it was way beyond my ability.

I didn't know what to do with the well either. It had long since become Daniel's toy. But he was already becoming bored with it. He was no longer throwing stones into its dark inner circle, along with objects he no longer wanted or was annoyed with because they had hurt him.

There was perhaps something I could do about the vegetable garden.

In a shed, I found a pick and a spade lying under a trunk. I also found a rake and pitchfork near the toilets. One cool summer's morning, I began to cut back the briar up to the place where onions, garlic, and tomatoes used to grow. I used the pick to dig up weeds, and then raked them up into a pile. With the spade I dug up the small, naked corner of earth and turned the soil over.

The next day I washed Daniel once again and we went in to Rosiori. The train whistle frightened me. The city, too. The crowds of people in a hurry, the packed streets, having to handle money and cross wide streets. All of this seemed almost new to me and so strange. Daniel asked me for ice cream on each streetcorner, as I window shopped greedily, scrutinizing every item I saw. I had the feeling that on the other side of the huge store windows the sales ladies were staring at me and making fun of me, of my curiosity. I experienced the same embarrassment, the same unease I had felt as a child when my mother took me into town before Easter to buy clothes, which I would wear for the holiday but then continue wearing for the rest of the year. Never in my life had I felt more humiliated that when my mother marched me past the counters asking for undershirts, underpants, and the cheapest shoes possible. I felt as if we were coming to display our poverty to these impudent and idiotic faces. Yet Mother was appreciative and snivelled any time anyone was the least bit polite to us.

In the cruel light of day, in the middle of the city, I realized how dirty I was. My arms and legs glistened with grime. I felt more comfortable at the big vegetable market. In the company of farmers, who wore frayed old clothing, amid piles of onions, where the smell of cheese was overpowering, I didn't look so impoverished. I bought a bunch of tomato plants and quickly returned to the train station. But we had just missed our train and the next one wasn't scheduled to leave for a few hours. I sat down on a bench, hanging on to my bags with my feet, as everyone else was doing, to keep them safe from thieves. Daniel fell asleep shortly, with his head on my lap.

I stared intently at the people who were walking by here and there. In one hand, they held a heavy bag and, in the other, they clung to the hand of a rambunctious and turbulent child trying to go off in all directions. As trains arrived and departed, other people flooded the platform and then deserted it. I would have liked to stay seated on that bench for my entire life, doing nothing and wanting nothing. Just watching.

Then, someone emerged from the crowd of strangers and said hello. It was a man who was thirty-five, perhaps forty, years old, dressed very simply, with greying hair, a plastic bag in his right hand and a bunch of newspapers under his arm.

It was George. George Popesco, a former classmate from primary school. We were both very embarrassed, especially me, because I had not recognized him at first glance. I had a hard time getting used to the way he looked, because he looked nothing like the pleasant boy I remembered. How had he grown old so suddenly? Why had he changed so drastically? He was miffed by my surprise too. In no time, our meeting became awkward. He didn't know whether we should sit down or remain standing. Every minute, he shifted his bag from one hand to the other. I looked him over from head to toe, trying to look happy, taking pains to show that I was glad to see him. I was happy, in fact, but the shock of meeting him, and especially of finding him so different, was so great that I could express no other emotion. A few long minutes elapsed, and George finally decided to sit down next to me on the uncomfortable wooden bench. In this position, with the light shining directly on me, it was his turn to be astonished. He could finally see my dirty skin and soiled, shabby, and washed-out clothing. I was sure that he could also get a whiff of my sour-smelling sweat, resulting from a long day of walking about town in the intense heat, not to mention the three-kilometre hike across the fields to get to the train station in the first place.

George looked at Daniel and me with tenderness. He told me about himself. He had been married for seven years but had no children. He didn't yet know whose fault it was. They hadn't been specially concerned with it, although they both wanted a child. He did not ask me what I was doing at the Rosiori train station, with tomato plants in my bag. He talked only about himself, not because he was conceited, but just because someone had to say something. He was working in Craiova as a dental technician. He had dreamed of becoming a doctor, encouraged by his mother and grandfather, who had been nurses in the village. He had failed the medical school entrance exam twice and had given up. Not long after, he had married a Jewish woman and had moved to Craiova.

George returned to our hometown two or three times a month. His parents' house was in the centre of the village, across from the general store. His mother was dead. He had never known his father. His half-sister was born out of the many risky affairs his mother had had, and she lived in Craiova as well. She worked in the archives, was married but also childless, and never went back to the family home, which was as old and uncomfortable as mine.

Each time he came, George would stay in the village for two days. He would work on the house, using all his skills and energy to prevent the decay from invading the property. He would use any material he could find to repair the roof, replacing the tiles that had been broken or blown off by the wind. He would rebuild the fence using planks of rotten wood or pieces of cardboard from boxes that he got from the nearby storekeeper. At the beginning, he would lock the house up carefully.

He would always bring his food from Craiova. He even showed me the contents of his bag, where I could see two plastic containers with red covers. Sometimes, to keep it simple, he just brought two fresh baguettes wrapped in newspaper. He would spend his evenings with the storekeeper, who had also been one of our classmates. They would go to the tavern together, order up two cold beers and then sit outside on the ground, at the edge of the old ditch that had been dug to drain the rainwater, now overgrown with quack grass.

A half hour later, we were talking about our childhood, about the times when he used to throw tomatoes at me and when I used to scratch his face with sandpaper. Together, we walked the three kilometres from the station to my house. He could have taken another route to get to the centre of the village, which would have been shorter and less tiring. He could have just taken the paved road that started behind the station where we got off, made a small loop, and then led directly to his house. I lived at the opposite end of the village and had to take a narrow, dusty road across the corn fields to get to my maternal grandparents' house. From there, I just had to take a little path to my house.

George put Daniel on his back and carried him like that the entire way. Daniel was knocked out by the heat. He leaned his head on George's shoulder and fell asleep. Around us, it was as silent as the grave. Even the wind had stopped blowing and the birds were no longer singing. Two acacia trees served as our landmarks. They had been planted with winter in mind, when snowstorms would cover footsteps. Workers who had to go from the village to town every day would sometimes get lost coming home, especially at night. We stopped and sat under the second tree, which had been half burned by lightning, and took off our shoes. Then we started walking again, with our bare toes immersed in a thick layer of burning dust, carrying our sandals in our hands. I was trying to protect the wilting tomato plants, while George was doing his best not to bounce about too much as he walked so as not to wake Daniel up. His forehead was drenched in sweat, but nothing would have made him stop carrying the child on his back.

We parted ways at the crossroads that marked the entrance to the hamlet where I was living. Before he left me, George invited me to go visit him and have a beer. I accepted.

Now that I had bought plants, I prepared the thirty-foot garden, which was divided into three rows with ten planting holes in each of them. I needed two buckets of water to water the seedlings and when the plants had grown bigger, three or even four. Only two of the seedlings dried out. I think an anthill had damaged the roots, but it had not affected the others.

I was so happy! For the first time since coming here, I could see the results of human efficiency. Every day, I would watch the slim stalks of the seedlings, with their little leaves quivering as they reached out to attach themselves to something, I would say to myself, "Anything is possible." Perhaps I would grow a vegetable garden, prune the grapevines, remove caterpillars from the trees, weed the garden, and make preserves. Then my mind would turn to really grandiose projects. Whitewashing the house or removing all the excess. There would only be one dwelling, my grandparents' house. The others, ugly and unnecessary, would be completely demolished, destroyed, and turned into dust. Let the grass grow and let the trees bear fruit. Let the garden be full of vegetables and my property prosper more than it had ever done before. I would cut the branches of the rosebush to make room for wildflowers, the ones that are so simple and discreet: four o'clock flowers, petunias, forget-me-nots, violets, and lion's head. Trees that were dried out and that bore no fruit would be cut down and replaced with the suckers growing out of their own trunks, because I didn't want to completely part with the fruits I had been used to since childhood.

Until I could carry out these ambitious projects, however, I would have to do something easier. I finally figured out what. I waited for a day when there was no wind. I took matches and set the big haystack on fire. The heap of dust burned for a long time. The organic matter had rotted and, inside, the hay was still moist. Daniel was delighted. He ran around the fire, so close to the flames that he was practically singed by them. For two days the embers kept their incandescent glow. I went outside every night in my nightgown and slippers to make sure the fire was not spreading. When all the embers burned out, I spread the ashes on the vineyard.

I was finally learning what an advantage it was to have a peasant background. I realized that I would survive, no matter what. I was not going to die of starvation or despair. I knew how to adapt to any situation, even the most inhospitable conditions.

I could make do with very little. I knew how to turn everything into an instrument, into a tool that could be put to good use. Like my ancestors, I had the extraordinary power to put my heart on ice and not give in to suffering. I never minded how shabby or desolate my surroundings were. I held on to whatever gave me strength. In the morning, I was happy if it was nice out, if the sun was shining in the sky and it was not raining. I had scoured my soul, erasing and eradicating all traces of painful weakness or sentimentality. I was like the widows of the area who lived in absolute solitude, without dying of fright, without being haunted or terrorized by ghosts.

Despite the nightmares that woke me up at night or the insomnia caused by the heat and mosquitoes, I was not afraid either—not of loneliness, the dark, or the future. As rundown as my property was, I wasn't scared by anything. My surroundings were so earthly, devoid of any mystery. The only secret I wondered about was their very existence. The trees, mosquitoes, little dog, and rats were all so real. There was nothing complicated about them. Nothing and no one could convince me that there was anything more to them, anything more than met the eye. I had tried, without success, to make more of them. A little mystery, something unexpected or surprising, would have broken up the deadly monotony of my life.

I remembered seeing my grandfather sitting in front of our door, on the trunk of an acacia tree, which replaced the bench that had been damaged by wind and rain over the course of many winters. He would lean his elbows on his knees and look down the road, from one end to the other, for hours and hours on end. Now it was my turn. I sat under the barren apple tree, watching Daniel, or the butterflies and birds swooping through the air. I wasn't thinking about anything, I no longer wished for anything.

This was my life and this was how it was going to be from then on.

August

In August, I had an unexpected and somewhat surprising visit.

A large well stood at the crossroads, with a drinking trough and an immense water wheel made of steel. My Aunt Cecilia had lived there. Along with my grandmother, the elderly woman with a heart condition was the sharpest memory I had from childhood. She was the only person, in my past and present, who knew how to tell a story. I had read many books, I had seen a pile of films, and I knew far too many stories, happy ones as well as sad ones. Aunt Cecilia belonged to that category of perfect screenwriters, who know the ending as soon as they have begun, but without letting you guess how things are going to turn out. Although she was illiterate, she had mastered the technique of *mise en abyme*. She had spent her childhood in another village, and then was practically bought by an old uncle and taken away against her will to the poorest place possible. She had married and spent her life with a man who had cheated on her from the very first night, and she had had terrible rows with her sisters-in-law over the fortune of her in-laws. All these tales had the sadness and pathos of good Slavic novels. She would come to our place every day, breathless, to tell us a new story or to follow-up on a previous one when her suspicions about her husband's adventures turned out to be true. She loved to spread the latest village rumours. In our little cluster of houses, she epitomized the malicious purveyor of gossip. Aunt Cecilia always knew—and she was seldom wrong—what was happening in everyone's kitchen, bedroom, bathroom, and basement. That's why no one liked her. By some quirk of fate, my family had accepted and adopted her. At our place, she felt at home, a sensation that had eluded her all her life. My grandmother, so restrained, so resistant to the charms of others, was drawn in by this woman's fairy tales. The only time I saw her full of enthusiasm was when she was listening to the jokes or dramas recounted in such detail by Aunt Cecilia. I had almost never seen my grandmother pay a visit to any of the women who lived nearby; nor was she happy when other people invited her over. The only neighbour for whom our door was always open was Cecilia, the woman who lived at the corner. My grandmother didn't lend anything to anyone and never asked anyone—except her daughters—for anything, not even a needle. She hated the community spirit that thrived among inhabitants of the village, a place where everyone knew exactly what the others owned or what they needed. Everyone was attuned to their neighbours' good fortunes or shortages, they knew about newly acquired possessions they coveted themselves: a sewing machine, an iron, an embroidery pattern.

Aunt Cecilia would drop in at any time of the day. Sometimes she would stay at our house from dawn to dusk; at other times, she would show up very late in the evening. If we were eating, she would take a spoon out of the drawer and sit down with us. The only person who grumbled about her unexpected visits was my grandfather who didn't like being disturbed at mealtime.

If he was annoyed, Aunt Cecilia could tell right away and would turn all her attention to him, her looks and smiles spurring sympathy, pity, and kindness as the old man mellowed.

From birth I had been the intended bride of her son, Ilie, who was seven years older than me. We had grown up with a very different idea of love. When I was in first grade, Ilie was already beginning to seduce young girls in the cornfields. It was clear to everyone that he was going to be tall when he grew up, whereas I was going to remain very small. I don't know if Ilie thought about me, if he had ever had any desire to marry me, but I had been in love with him forever and wanted to grow up as fast as possible to become his wife. Especially since you had to live with your husband's mother, according to the village customs. In those days, I couldn't imagine things happening any other way.

I had always been flattered by Aunt Cecilia's attention and approval. She would often say that I was the most beautiful, the most hard-working, the cleanest of all the girls. That's the way I grew up, admired by two elderly women.

During my childhood, I had rarely said more than a few words to Ilie. But I knew that he listened to his mother and that he would follow her advice. I was thus certain about one thing, which was inevitable, and which required no input from me. When he was fourteen years old, however, he went away to the lycée, and we were separated for good. After Aunt Cecilia died, I never saw him again, not even during the holidays. I often heard bad things about him. He had turned out to be frivolous and a womanizer. When I was taking the entrance exams for university, my mother told me that he had married a young woman from a neighbouring village and that he now lived in Bucharest. I once thought I spotted him in front of the Victoria department store, with a woman who barely came up to his shoulders.

One hot August evening, Ilie appeared, looming on the other side of the small garden gate. I was sitting on a low stool in the middle of the yard washing Daniel in his galvanized steel tub. I caught sight of Ilie and recognized him instantly. He was a particularly handsome man, with black hair, red lips, a delicate nose, and slanted eyes like the Mongols, recessed beneath arched eyebrows. He hadn't changed at all. He had the same seductive look in his eyes, which I recalled with excitement.

With each step he took toward me, I grew more unsettled, more embarrassed, and more afraid. I was as moved as I had been in my younger days, when it made me happy just to be near him. My hands were immersed in soapy water. I quickly dried them off on my blouse, but Ilie didn't offer to shake my hand. Instead, he kept his hands on his hips, looking amused at seeing me like this. Daniel was content to keep splashing around. Paying no attention to the stranger, he just asked me to leave him alone in the tub, so he could keep playing with the rubber duckies I had snatched away from him.

The two of us went into the veranda. Because of the big windows without curtains, the temperature had shot up in there and it felt like a hothouse. I brought out two small chairs and we sat down. I apologized for having nothing to give him to eat or drink, except a few overripe cherries. But he just wanted to stare at me, directly and greedily, not at all shy and obviously astonished to find me here as if it were the ends of the earth. We were sweating profusely. I stole a look at him and tried not to seem surprised. I was taken with the very virile way he was seated on the chair, which had been occupied only by my grandfather, his legs spread open and his elbows on his knees. I could make out his testicles, falling loosely in the crotch of his pants, touching the edge of the wooden chair. Very quickly, Ilie started to question me indiscreetly about why I was here. He answered his own question,

"Your husband? Is it because of him?"

He had the same peasant mentality as our parents, who believed that all change was brought about by something bad that had happened. Ilie was not as discreet as George, who had kept quiet about any improper suspicions he might have had.

"Yes," I answered.

"Was he cheating on you?"

"Yes."

"Oh, if only you had been willing to marry me!"

For more than ten years, I had wondered why my childhood dream had not come to pass. Whose fault was it? Had Ilie ever been aware of his mother's intentions? Sometimes I suspected that Aunt Cecilia had not shared her secret plans with anyone but me and that she had matched us up without the consent of her son. Our marriage had been dreamed up to suit her rather than us. All the poor woman wanted was to not die alone, abandoned like a stray dog, the way she had lived her life. Most of her fears were actually well founded. She died in the hospital, without any candles lit at her bedside, which for a religious person meant eternal damnation. My mother had told me everything not long after her chaotic funeral. When she was brought home for the burial, her corpse reeked because it had been poorly embalmed after the autopsy, and her flesh was so swollen and disfigured that no one would come near her. Except for my mother, who had no sense of smell. Moved by their former friendship and urged on by my grandmother, my mother was insensitive to the divine significance of all this decay. She had tried to dress the rotting body in appropriate clothing but had to give up after a piece of flesh came off in her hand. The village women felt avenged for the contempt in which Aunt Cecilia had held everyone all her life and for the nasty rumours she had spread about them. Sitting on wooden benches, they kept watch for the priest out in the yard so they could observe his demeanor and scold him if they detected the least sign of disgust.

Ilie had never looked for me, even though we were living in the same city. When I was attending the lycée, he was a professional football player, despite the fact that his mother looked down on what she considered to be an occupation without prestige. He even played in the top division. He fractured his leg during a championship match, however, and was forced to give up playing. While I was at university, he was working in a greenhouse growing vegetables. I heard all these things from my mother. Each time I went home on vacation, Ilie would be the first person I was interested in, the first I would ask after, even before inquiring about how all my family members were doing. And this continued even after he got married.

Then the inevitable happened. An erotic spark flared up between us, sending a wave of warmth through our bodies, a sign that we would eventually sleep together. How? Where? It was only a question of time. The infinite solitude around us elicited deep feelings, too. We were both on the edge of an orgasm without having touched each other. I had a burning sensation in my belly. Ilie would not stop staring at me. He looked me directly in the eye, he wasn't shy, he wasn't ashamed. He kept on talking to me, but what he was saying didn't matter. His words were merely an extension of the sexual passion that was growing between us. We talked about mundane things. Ilie asked me what Daniel and I ate, where we slept, but he was surely thinking of other things. In what part of the house were we going to make love, what part of my body would he penetrate, where would I feel his burning breath and moist lips, and when was he going to fondle my breasts?

Outside, Daniel was still talking to his plastic figures. Ilie was unconcerned as he looked at the child splashing water on his pyjamas, which were laid out on the little chair next to the bathtub. He didn't have children. He didn't want any either, although he was married for the second time. He was old enough for his paternal instincts to have been offset by the more selfish desire to live freely, all alone, without the heartache that comes with raising kids. Nothing is more painful than the excessive care our parents take of us, the way they worry about how we live our life, about what our future will look like. Even if they are unable to offer us any kind of help, they suffer needlessly if we happen to fail. Relations between parents and their offspring often morph, first of all, into a friendly cross-examination, then into advice grounded in ancestral wisdom, ending with laments about our lack of gratitude, our stupidity, and our misfortunes.

The sun was about to set. The tiled roofs that could be seen above the big oven were bathed in a reddish glow. I got up to take Daniel out of the cold bathwater.

Ilie stood in the narrow doorway of the veranda and squeezed my arm. As he gripped my flesh, he told me that he had to go. His wife didn't know where he had gone. And he did not invite me to his house. Out of an almost evil instinct I realized that she, the third person in this story, should not know that I was here. Ilie and I were locked into the circle of our guilty desires, closely tied to this place. We had formed a pact of wickedness, of dark and mysterious desires, from which strangers, like those in the Bible, were excluded. Others remained on the periphery of this world.

Ilie told me that he would return to the village as often as he could. His father was still alive but, since the death of Aunt Cecilia, he was living with his eldest son in the city of Drobeta. After his wife passed away, his health had declined, although he refused to admit what was happening to him. Ilie was the only one in the family who went to the trouble of maintaining the vineyard and the vegetable garden. In the summer, he would drive from Bucharest twice a month; in the winter, he came only once, to pick up his bottles of wine before Christmas. He had not known that I was here until he saw me at the well. When he was leaving, Ilie assured me that we would see each other again the same day.

I didn't sleep a wink all night. I waited for Ilie until dawn, listening carefully for him. During those long, suffocating hours, I was overcome by all kinds of emotion. I went back over our encounter in the most minute detail, and I came up with an ending to the story. If Daniel had not been there, my eternal fiancé would have lifted my skirt up, pushed me up against the brick wall that enclosed the patio, and held me in his arms. I did not want to see his hard penis, not even in my imagination.

This was how I drew the line, creating a kind of screen out of a sense of modesty.

A little after midnight, I thought I heard an unfamiliar sound. It wasn't the wind and it wasn't the cats. After so many nights of silence and insomnia, I had learned to distinguish the sounds of birds twittering, the dog breathing, mice gnawing on the wooden beams, moths nibbling on the clothing. This time it was something I was unaccustomed to. I went down, but without stepping out onto the veranda. I stood there a long time, without moving, watching the small garden gate. No one was there.

The following day was Sunday. A brief rain shower had cooled off the morning, but it had not rained enough to wash away the layer of dust. The wet leaves on the trees had taken on a cheery springtime sheen. I didn't want to be seen so I didn't leave the yard. I was going to keep the meeting with Ilie quiet, secret. I felt guilty and at the same time I would have done anything to satisfy my shameful desires, to not let this opportunity for a tryst elude me. How could I think that the other woman, my rival, would invite me for a coffee when I wanted to make love with her husband? She would easily guess as much immediately, just by looking at my face. How could you free such a man from her clutches? Before sundown I heard the sound of a car driving down the road. I ran to the door, but all I saw was a thick cloud of dust.

They were gone! Ilie had not even bothered to say goodbye. He didn't care about me, he was as callous as he had always been. I was scrawny, I had been deceived by my husband, I was filthy, sweaty, alone with a runny-nosed child. How could he fall in love with me? It wasn't even worth being polite to such a woman. I longed for his affection, just as I had when I was fifteen, but it was no use.

On Monday afternoon I walked through the wrought-iron gate into their yard. I was not likely to be seen. The only person who still lived around there was an old woman, about ninety years old, a person whom my grandmother once suspected of being her husband's mistress, before the war, when he rode around on a white horse to the great delight of all the village girls. The house was a bit lower down in the valley, but the windows faced the other side of the road. The gate had an apple tree on each side. It was wired shut, not to keep strangers out but rather to keep it attached to the wall. In the yard, I could detect tire tracks in the dust, which had hardened with the light rain that had fallen the day before. I walked along the little path with quack grass sprouting out of the cracks. The first autumn leaves had fallen onto the patio stones. The door to the house was locked with a big rusty padlock. The vines were ripening, well-tended with the canes carefully trained along metal trellises. I picked a basket of grapes and headed back nibbling on bunches of unwashed fruit.

I had only been in this yard a few times in my entire life. Aunt Cecilia would come to our house every day, but, like my grandmother, I visited her only rarely. Her house felt a bit "citified," with small touches added by her eldest son, not to mention the fact that my aunt used to do all her cooking, ironing, and even all the washing indoors. Aunt Cecilia had inherited the custom of eating breakfast from her slightly bourgeois family. She would serve tea and little cookies that she had baked in her gas oven. She always kept little biscuits on a table in her bedroom. The water glasses in her house were always covered with a napkin, to keep the flies and dust off.

From the age of seven, when Aunt Cecilia told me that I was going to be her daughter-in-law, I always felt like a young lady when I went to her house. My physical features were not striking enough to appeal to Ilie, who liked beautiful and attractive girls. On the other hand, I thought that my shyness was an advantage, that it would make me more appealing. I had no choice but to act like a well-brought-up, superior young lady, who would retire to her boudoir while my beloved played football or frolicked with the big girls, hiding in the cornfields to make love. After all my determination to win him over, to make him love me, I was doomed to remain unnoticed and unappreciated.

Despite Ilie's unforgiveable departure, I continued to wait for him, although I felt guilty and ashamed of the thoughts swirling around in my head.

In our little world, everything related to sex was regarded as unpardonable behaviour. Fraud, theft, lies, and even crimes were merely senseless, sometimes necessary, mistakes. But no sin was more serious than adultery, since it could compromise a person for all time.

A married woman who cheated on her husband lost her dignity for her entire life. It became risky for her to appear in public and she no longer spoke with any authority, not even to a small child. Nothing was more vulnerable or more shameful than the lower part of the body. Despite the coarseness, even the vulgarity of colloquial speech, sexual relations here were shrouded in profound prudishness. It was obvious that these sexual morals had kept this world alive. In the big cities, love had become a kind of gymnastics, while here it was still considered a fundamental feeling. The decline had started when taboo had turned into ungodliness, an unfortunate change fuelled by alcohol. Shame was clouded over by fumes that evaporated from strong liquor. Drunkenness had made everything easier. In the last years of her life, my mother had had many lovers. Younger, single fifty-year-old women slept with anyone and everyone who offered to do so, with the few remaining men who were still active enough. They were as voracious as female spiders who devour the males after mating. Casually formed couples got drunk and jumped into bed together in the filthiest places, except in a bed itself, which remained like an altar, the last thing they wished to defile. The morning after, they could no longer look each other in the eye, but once evening set in, the story would repeat itself. They did not even have the decency to keep their adventures a secret. There were no longer any prohibitions. There were no morals and no God. Total nihilism ruled.

I, on the other hand, had reverted to my ancestral sentiments. Of course, I wanted to have sex, but I was ashamed to admit it. Since seeing Ilie again, the things I touched smelled like sperm to me. Commonplace objects became erotic ones, transformed into icons of heightened sexuality. I saw phallic symbols everywhere and my body took on a postcoital odour. On my hands I could smell the perfume of men I had once touched.

After Ilie stood me up, my urge to fix things up disappeared forever. The work I had done until then seemed almost useless to me. The tomato plants had grown but they bore very little fruit. Here and there a few small tomatoes clung to the vines. Though they weren't ripe yet, I amused myself by persistently keeping the birds from pecking at them. Besides, I had done almost nothing but work in the vegetable garden. The dilapidated structures and fallow grounds had benefited in no way from my presence, which should have been lively and active. No smoke curled up the chimney. I didn't cook, I didn't do laundry, and I didn't sweep up the yard. I made very little difference to the smells, the silence or the squawking of birds. Daniel's games were also very subdued. His presence was even more discreet, more imperceptible than mine. For days on end, our sustenance was the overripe fruit that fell from the trees, which Daniel picked and ate, worms and all. He was afraid to climb up onto the branches because of the giant caterpillars, which he was content to poke at with a stick from underneath. He would disappear almost all day long into the vineyard, in search of little grapes nestling among the intertwined tendrils that still bore fruit. Once, he brought me the skin of a dead snake, half eaten by ants. Daniel loved to touch all manner of small animals, whether they were soft, sticky, filthy, or slimy. After it rained, he would collect the earthworms that poked their heads out of the ground. He held on to both ends and pulled until they split apart. Then he emptied the contents and wiped off the gluey mixture of guts and dirt onto his pants. My son had a penchant for all things wretched, filthy, and sordid, something he did not get from me. I have always felt out of place living here, where mice, frogs, lizards, crickets, and beetles were rampant, even indoors.

All things considered, I felt that love, or the anticipation of love, was going to confer new meaning on my stay here. My fervent desire to be loved by Ilie, loved to death, really reminded me of my past, when censored films tickled my imagination without completely satisfying it. For a long time, I was mystified by girls who kissed a guy on the mouth and immediately got pregnant, without further explanation. Such innocent images, projected on black and white television sets, would send shivers up my spine. Why was there no one to punish me for my wet dreams or for pretending that my nightgown was a low-cut dress revealing my tiny breasts? I still believe that no one feels more guilty than a ten-year-old girl overcome by wild impulses before falling asleep. I still ached with the memory of those days, burning with the shame of my juvenile fantasies.

One day, Aunt Joana, my father's last living sister, abruptly awakened me from the erotic reveries into which I had fallen after Ilie left. Her unexpected appearance magnified my shame and feelings of guilt. It didn't make sense, because my aunt should have had nothing to do with the thoughts that haunted me. She had known for some time about my strange goings-on that summer, but she had been waiting for me to visit her first. Now, she was coming to ask whether I needed anything. Perhaps she could bake some bread for me, it would be better than what was available in the stores, which she had always found dense and bitter. She had brought me two baguettes baked directly on the bricks of her fireplace. She also offered to supply me with cheese regularly because she still kept two goats and three sheep. But then, she remembered that I didn't eat cheese, even before I reminded her about it. My mother thought that I might be sick because I rejected this mythical food, which had saved our people from famine so often but which didn't agree with me. I would not sit down at the table until everyone else had finished eating cheese, which was served at the beginning of every meal—breakfast, lunch, and supper. My grandmother would take the foul-smelling platter away and hide it in the cupboard while my mother began to serve soup to my grandfather and then my father.

My aunt's visit cheered me up immensely. She was the only one of my father's sisters to whom I had felt somewhat close as a child. Unlike my other aunts, who were severe looking, Aunt Joana was rather benevolent, with the understated kindness you might expect from a childless woman.

The paternal side of my family was well known for its standoffishness, a quality embodied by my grandmother. They were all selfish, stingy, and solitary. Even new members of the family quickly adopted this attitude. The women of the family banded together to avoid mixing with strangers or neighbours. No one wanted to make friends, have any visitors, or confide in other people. Everything that happened in the family stayed in the family. Unlike other women born before or during the Second World War, my father's sisters had gone to school. All four of them had been good students, and the priest, who was also the village teacher, liked them a lot, especially Marie, the eldest, who was said to be very gifted. But, according to custom, their parents had to marry them off quickly. The priest paid a special visit to my grandparents' house on behalf of Marie. Dressed in his long black robe, he begged them to have pity on their daughter and send her to the city. But nothing came of it. Although the priest had been unsuccessful in his efforts, Aunt Marie stubbornly opposed her parents and fought for the right to stay in school. My grandmother was forced to hide her shoes from her, but that didn't prevent Marie from going to school anyway, barefoot. The arrival of winter put an end to that battle. For the following six months, the boots of the entire family were also hidden. After that, Aunt Marie was married off to a boy who was a little too fat, but who would become the village tax collector, because he knew how to write. It actually turned out to be a good marriage. Throughout her life, Aunt Marie carefully conserved paper on which she would write out thousands and thousands of numbers, a task with which her husband had entrusted her.

The maternal side of my family was totally different from the paternal branch. My mother's brothers were generous, almost foolishly so. They were also feeble-minded and dimwitted. They liked to go to parties, get drunk, and pick fights. On their way home from the tavern, they would sing loudly, waking up almost the entire village. They liked to show off their strength and masculinity, fundamental qualities in a man. They had the utmost contempt for those who were sickly. Being intelligent was worth nothing next to muscle power. They did like to read adventure stories, however. On weekends, at naptime, they would thumb through books like Karl May's *Winnetou* or Alexandre Dumas's *The Three Musketeers*—for the umpteenth time. They had but one hero, and that was Superman.

I felt comfortable with my maternal uncles, but I admired my father's sisters. In my presence, the four women had a rigidity that intimidated me. People who were extremely serious scared me, but, at the same time, they made me feel safe. The members of my family did not like each other. They nevertheless had a tribal mentality, rooted in solidarity, which was paramount.

We would work and party together, as a family. Christmas and Easter were celebrated at our house, revolving around my grandmother. And when there was something to be done in the vegetable garden or the vineyard, everyone would come over, in which case we wasted more time setting the dinner tables and cleaning up.

In those days, I didn't pay visits to anyone except Aunt Joana. My cousins perpetuated their parents' aversion to me. Because I didn't have brothers and didn't work as hard as their kids, my aunts considered me flighty. My only consolation was that my grandmother loved me more. She cared much less for her seven other grandchildren and eleven great-grandchildren. The younger kids, in particular, got on her nerves. Every time they came to visit, Grandma would watch them like a hawk to make sure they didn't touch or pocket anything.

After my grandparents died, the family split apart. My mother had never made a good impression. In their opinion, she was much too generous and a bit simple-minded. Even worse, she liked to drink and would get drunk often. My aunts had inherited Grandma's disapproval of this kind of family and background, but in this case their disapproval was just directed at my mother. They only criticized her in the privacy of their homes, when they got together on certain occasions. It was very painful for my father to see his wife rejected like that. Sometimes he went to see his sisters on his own, and was well treated, like an orphan. My aunts had no idea how hard it was to live with my mother. In any case, these women, who were a lot older than my mother, would never have believed how lazy my father was and how little he did at home now that he was retired.

Aunt Joana started asking me questions right away, just as Ilie had done. From the outset, she had guessed that I had left my husband. But what was I looking for? When would I go back to my husband? How did I expect to get by, all alone with a child? How could I raise a child without a father?

I was grateful to her for trying to talk to Daniel, whom she was meeting for the first time. She was worried about his weak constitution and deeply touched by the fate of a fatherless child. She had never been a mother herself and, in her view, children suffered all the time and were a burden and source of unhappiness to their parents. She was sure that so much deprivation was torture for the little guy. She thought the place I was living in was cursed. Although hers was no better, my ramshackle house, which had gone to rack and ruin, was not a suitable home for anyone except ghosts and scary revenants.

Of all my aunts, Aunt Joana was the only one with whom I had had a special relationship. The others looked upon me as a kind of parasite, living in the company of four grown-ups who were content to serve me and who never asked me to do anything, not even fetch a glass of water. She was the only one I wasn't afraid of, with whom I was even able to have a conversation. She lived in a house next to the high school in the centre of the village, where I had done my last four years of schooling before leaving for the lycée. During winter storms, when I was unable to walk the three kilometres to get home, I would stay with my uncles for several days, even weeks. Aunt Joana had a lot of trouble getting used to having me there and didn't like having me around at first. Her husband,

Uncle Jon, was a great help. He was the only one to show some warmth toward me, so that when the time came to leave again, once the weather had improved, my aunt even invited me to stay on a few more days. But at the beginning it had been difficult for me to live with them. My aunt was not used to washing, feeding, or caring for a child. Having a third person in the house was quite a burden. I was lucky that my uncle was there. When we watched television together, he would pretend that he didn't understand the big words, which he mangled so much that even Aunt Joana would burst out laughing. Even though she scowled at me, I began to feel at home after a few days.

I especially liked how big the rooms were. They had been smart enough to live in the big house, rather than the outbuildings. Because they had no children, they weren't preoccupied with making money or wasting it. They were comfortable and relatively affluent. At their house, I could eat white bread, spread with butter and honey, which I liked more than anything in those days.

Their house was also typical of this particular region in the South. There was a large vestibule with three large wooden doors leading to the bedrooms and kitchen. Attached to the main building were sheds, but these were small storage areas. Except for breakfast, they took their meals in the house, at a small round wooden table with three small chairs.

Their house didn't have garish paintings on shelves, in drawers, or on the walls, as we did in our house. Aunt Joana was too old to be fond of enamel knick-knacks, stuffed dogs and cats, glass roosters and fish, plastic vases, or nylon checkered tablecloths, items she particularly disapproved of because they were costly. Her walls were covered with hangings made from real wool, linen, or hemp fabric, with simple geometric patterns, which had been part of her dowry when she got married. Red and black cotton headscarves were draped over authentic icons, which were painted on glass or wood. The only pictures hanging on the walls were sepia photos of my uncle's family.

At night, Aunt Joana would give me one of her husband's long cotton nightshirts to wear, rolled up at the neck and the sleeves. My uncle wore pyjamas and would change the top twice a night because of an illness that made him sweat profusely.

The main attraction of their house was the cuckoo clock. I was also fascinated by an enormous ball made of hair elastics decorated with plastic beads. My uncle's sister worked in Bucharest, in a factory that manufactured plastics, and she was the one who had brought them. Even though I cried and pleaded with her, my aunt wouldn't let me have one single elastic. She suggested that I make pigtails, which she offered to braid with red yarn.

Now, after so many years, my aunt was scolding me as if she were my mother. But I wasn't angry. Far from it. Her strict manner did me good; she made me feel a bit safer. Her reaction to my misfortunes even brought tears to my eyes. For the first time, I was upset by my situation. Talking to my aunt, I was not afraid to express my feelings and show sadness I hadn't yet been conscious of.

And then… perhaps I really was unhappy.

As she was leaving, we decided that she would bake bread every Friday to last me the entire week. At the same time, she would also give me a small piece of cheese for my son, who didn't have the same aversion to it as I did.

Cheese, after all, was a noble food that was universally appreciated, except by the Turks. My aunt had inherited my grandmother's customs and convictions. For these women, everything that was bad for our people derived from the former Ottoman Empire. As a final word, my aunt advised me once again to stop acting like a Turk, which in our language denoted stubbornness, and to go back to my husband as quickly as possible.

On the doorstep, and before turning her slim back, Aunt Joana told me to go look under the hay in the farthest shed. She remembered that my father had hidden a bicycle there, and that it was still in good condition. If I needed it, I could use it. This was the only machine that my aunt accepted, without totally approving of women who used them.

My aunt's visit left a deep impression on me. An image of the old lady was embedded in my memory, her widow's headscarf framing her parchment face. Each time I thought of Ilie, she was there, looking at me with the same hard eyes as my grandmother, with no sympathy for the frailties of the flesh. I tried my best to erase both women from my mind, but they stubbornly hung on. As soon as I began to fantasize about making love with Ilie, the memory of my aunt would take hold. I would imagine her bent over her oven, whistling for her sheep, removing kernels of corn with a metal peeler, chopping up beets for the pigs, feeding sick lambs with a baby bottle, gathering nettles for the ducklings, or mending shirts worn out at the elbows. I was as solitary as a cuckoo, but my cheeks were on fire.

Aunt Joana was right. My father's bicycle was there, well hidden. The chain and the mudguard were a bit rusty, but the bike was still in good condition. After cleaning off the dust and dirt, I put a bit of cooking oil on the gears. I looked everywhere until I found a pump, which I used for putting air in the tires.

I rode around the deserted roads, from one end of the village to the other, leaving clouds of dust behind me. I was as happy as back in the days when my mother taught me to ride a bike. I felt completely free. When I went by the same house for the second time, people hardly ever peeked out of their doorways to watch me ride by. I wasn't bothering them. They were no longer surprised at anything.

I left the village, rode past the cemetery where my parents were buried, and got lost on the vast plains. The fields were carefully cultivated. The farmers had joined cooperatives, from which they received practically nothing, but they were still happy now that they didn't have to worry about planting or harvesting. There wasn't a soul around. Suddenly, I thought I spotted a black silhouette on the horizon. It was a vague, mysterious sort of creature. I immediately rode toward it, but it was only a plastic bag that had been blown up and carried by the wind.

I went back home at nightfall. Daniel had not even noticed that I was gone. As usual, he was dirty, with snot all over his face, his hair covered in dust, his mouth stained red by the sour cherries he had eaten, his fingernails filthy. His underpants, which was the only piece of clothing he had on, had grown yellow with time. His pecker, the size of a little finger, poked its head out at the top of one leg. He lived outside from morning to night, baking in the blazing sun, which didn't do him any harm. He looked good, brown as a berry. He even slept under the burning rays. He had become a child of the Earth. He needed very little sustenance. He slept a lot and otherwise needed nothing. All he asked of me was to be allowed to play with his rubber duckies in the evening as he soaked in his bathtub full of water that had been heated by the sun. He didn't need my supervision, although one time he gave me a terrible scare.

I had never forbidden him to leave the yard. And actually, he had never shown any desire to do so. One day, however, I couldn't find him. I called out to him, I shouted his name for several hours, I looked everywhere, even in the loft which he wouldn't have been able to reach anyway, because there was no ladder. Then, I left the yard. First of all, I rushed to the big well. The mirror of water shining deep down at the bottom of the hole had always been a source of anguish for all parents. When I was a child, the worst threat was, "I am going to throw you into the well." Every time a child disappeared, people would immediately suspect that he or she had fallen in by accident or else had been thrown in by an enemy seeking revenge. I leaned over the crumbling concrete basin and yelled, "Yoo-hoo!" Nothing. I then started to wander up and down the few nearby streets, knowing that he couldn't have gone anywhere else. But after a few hours, I found myself much farther out, in the valley, on the banks of a stream that flowed through the village. The riverbed was empty of water at this time of year, full of rusty cans and pails, bones left by dogs and cats, broken glass. Yard waste had been carted down to the edge of the little stream and dumped there to rest in the riverbed too. The dry cracked earth crunched underfoot as I walked over it.

I was extremely tired when I returned to the village. Nonetheless, as time passed and sunset drew near, instead of worrying, I grew calmer. I was sure that Daniel had just wandered off. He had probably gone into one of the abandoned houses and, when he left, had turned the wrong way. Instead of heading toward our yard, he had likely walked toward the edge of the village. I told myself that nothing terrible could happen to him.

For the first time, I wanted to ask one of my neighbours for help. A little farther down, there was a house that still looked lived in, despite the menacing bushes in the yard. However, I absolutely could not remember who lived there.

Without calling out directly, I entered the yard, which was overgrown with weeds, the most invasive of which was creeping bent grass. A little path led to the back of the property. Shading my eyes with my hands, I peered into the bedroom window. As I leaned forward, I grazed myself with metal wires that were used to hold the posts together. The inside of the house was in total darkness and I needed a few seconds to get used to it. Two thin figures appeared to be struggling in the bed. I went in immediately without knocking. As soon as I stepped inside, I was struck by a strong smell of urine. In the bedroom there was only one bed, as well as a table and chair. Someone had drilled a hole through the centre of the bed and placed a bucket underneath. An old woman had stuck one leg through the hole leaving the other one hanging outside the bed. Behind her was an old man, who had only one hand and eyes curiously covered with a white cloth. He was trying as hard as he could to get her out, all the while uttering terrible curses.

“Leave me alone, you are going to kill me,” cried the old woman.

"But you have to pee. Why aren't you doing anything?"

I took the other leg of the woman and I pulled. The old man moaned unceasingly. Blood was streaming from his eyes from the effort. The old lady stared at me stupidly.

Finally, I remembered them. The woman's name was Iulika while the villagers had nicknamed the man "One-Arm," because he had lost his right hand during the war. Now Iulika was confined to her bed, almost paralyzed and her husband had been completely blind for fifteen years. The man had sensed that a stranger was there. While his wife watched me, frightened, he sniffed in my direction. He took a deep breath, like a dog, and covered his ears.

He kept asking his wife, "Who is here? Tell me, who is it? Is it Nikulina?"

"No, it's not Nikulina. It's not her."

The bucket underneath the bed was full of urine. When she fell the old lady had wet her skirt in the stinking liquid. Now she was trying to wring it out by hand and keep it away from her skin. I took the bucket and emptied it out at the back of the yard; then I put it back in its original place. Without saying anything else, I left and quickly ran down the main road.

Was there anyone left who still wanted to discover a new world among the stars? Thousands of messages, translated into all the languages of the world, were blasted up into the ether. For whom? Weren't we fed up with our misery yet? Weren't we in enough of a mess as it was? The blind, the paralyzed, urine, garbage?

I didn't know what to do anymore. Keep on looking or go home? Several seconds ticked by laboriously under the burning afternoon sun. I then decided to go to the far end of the village, with my clothing now permeated with the persistent odour of urine. For a time, a dog followed me along the deserted and sunny streets. I had trouble recognizing the little doggie who had left us a month before. He hadn't been sorry to leave, for he had also found us pathetic.

I don't know how long I spent walking around like that. As if I were hallucinating, I remembered stopping in front of a house that had been cut in two vertically. One part had fallen down while the other was still standing, resembling anatomical models that show a cross-section of the insides of a human body. You could still see a window, the doorframe, and a broken-down stove. In the yard, among the briars, stood two apple trees full of caterpillars. The part of the house that had remained standing looked the way it had ten years before. When they broke up, the couple living there had chosen to separate their goods that way. After several years of torture, the wife had decided to leave her drunkard of a husband and had taken half their possessions while leaving the other half to him. Because it was impossible to live there, he had moved into his parents' cottage in a little valley when they died. He had been found there, dead drunk, a year before my father passed away.

I gave up my search, for the day. Daniel would come back home on his own. He would surely find his way. I was so tired that I could no longer think straight. In the evening, before going to bed, I patrolled the house several times, from one door to the other, just to kill time. I looked down the lane to the left, to the right, even after the sun set, when it was no longer possible to see anything clearly.

I resumed my search the following morning at dawn, not because I was worried or distressed, but rather because I had nothing else to do. I cupped my hands around my mouth, like a megaphone, and called out. But no one answered. I had a headache and suddenly realized that I hadn't eaten anything since the previous day.

At one time, there had been a little stand, built against the fence of the doctor's house, where bread was sold. There had once been an acacia tree in this spot, but it had been chopped down. The tree stump now had smooth bark, a sign that it had been used as a bench for a long time. My grandfather would sit there with his elbows on his knees, waiting, with the women and children, for the wagon that delivered the bread. The baker, who drove the delivery cart himself, served my grandfather first, handing the bread to him over all the little heads. A wrought-iron cross was planted in the ground near the acacia, leaning slightly into the wind. Two initials and a date were engraved on the cross. That was where the most terrible event of my childhood had occurred. The most terrible, because a crime had been committed.

It happened on a Sunday. I remember Sunday stories very well. It was the day that I was given the nasty job of driving the geese out to pasture. The rest of the week the geese were my grandfather's business. But on Sunday, when it was time for the geese to be taken out, the old man was carrying out the complicated process of shaving. He started in the morning by sharpening his old razor on a leather belt he had inherited from his father for this purpose. A little bowl of boiled water, a piece of paper on which he collected the residue of lather mixed with beard hair clippings, and the soap that he rubbed slowly onto the thinning shaving brush were all part of the ritual, which had taken on so much importance in our family that everyone had to interrupt their work to devote themselves to it. We were all inconvenienced by the place chosen for this operation. My grandfather would sit on a tall stool, in front of a mirror that had almost no silver left on the back. He would remain there, immobile, ceremoniously calling for each object to be brought to him. My father even added newspaper, very nervous since Grandpa stubbornly clung to the traditional straight razor instead of using the new kind made by Gillette.

On that particular Sunday, as I was coming back to the house, herding the gaggle of squawking geese and trying to keep the gander from biting me, I realized that something very serious was going on in our village. I left the geese mid-way along the path—that's how my family lost five of them, actually—and began to head toward the crossroads. A woman was screaming. Everyone was running to the place, beside the doctor's big house. I left our own street and could see that a crowd was gathering and forming a large circle around the crossroads. As I drew closer, I became very worried. In my hand I clutched the stick that I had been using to fend off the gander. My mother had seen me from a distance and took me aside to tell me to go home. Then, out of curiosity, she went back into the crowd again, sure that I had followed her instructions.

From the middle of the circle, you could hear a woman moaning. I didn't understand what was going on, until Paula, a young neighbour, told me the story. She had arrived a little earlier than I, but she hadn't been able to see anything either. Children were prevented from getting into the middle of the circle. But she had heard that Mattei Bratu's son had killed someone whose name she couldn't remember. Beyond the dense wall of people, there was a dead man, whose throat had been slit with a knife. Beside him lay the killer, his hands tied together with rope. The cries of the old woman, the young victim's mother, now began to make sense. All around, people were whispering about a love story that had unfolded in the community of shepherds at the far end of the village. Mother again stepped out of the crowd. This time, it was too mobbed for her to see me. Paula and I had hidden in the doctor's yard. We had taken shelter under the chicken coop, where we met my cousin Adrian and his neighbour Gheorghe. They gave us the gory details. Adrian confirmed that the corpse's neck had been severed and that the head was swimming in blood. He told us that after having been stabbed, the man did not die instantly but had continued to talk to his killer, who had been his best friend. They were both very drunk and had fought over a woman, the killer's sister. Then we heard the police car, followed by a cloud of dust and a pack of vicious dogs. The villagers began to drift away. We left our hiding place to get closer. A few men were wrestling with a blood-stained old woman who was tearing her hair out and refusing to get out of the way. A wooden cart was then seen leaving the middle of the circle and heading toward the hamlet where the shepherds lived. As it rolled along, blood dripped from the corpse and stained the dusty earth in its tracks. The police car drove off to the centre of the village. I thought I caught a glimpse of a bearded face through the car window, a face that I associated with the young man who would sometimes clean out the sediment in our well.

I'm positive that I saw traces of blood on the village square, which had now emptied out. But each time I passed the cross, I would only remember the time when the four of us had hidden under the doctor's chicken coop, awaiting the outcome, afraid but so very curious.

This story had nothing to do with me. I felt, however, that the rusty cross represented the link between those who had once been inside the circle and those who had remained on the outside. Between those who had just heard people talking about tears and blood and those who had been close by, close enough to have touched them.

All the terror I felt as a result of my son's disappearance was dwarfed by the memory of that event. Instead of fear, I now felt rage, rage against the little tyke. Looking for him had awakened these disturbing images, which I had long since put out of my mind and which I had studiously avoided thinking about until now. I had managed to avoid being crushed by the memory. I had succeeded in preserving my past, my childhood, in making them bearable. And, suddenly, they resurfaced the way they once were, intact. Searching amid the wreckage, looking for my child, was like excavating my own past. It was impossible to satisfy my curiosity, once it had been sparked.

I climbed onto the acacia stump on which my grandfather had sat, waiting for the bread cart to arrive. I peeked inside the doctor's yard. The door of the old chicken coop was barricaded by a bundle of dried branches. I touched the wooden pickets of the fence, which the doctor used to coat with a petroleum-based product to keep the wood from rotting, making the fence disastrous for our clothes. By now, the wood was dried out and darkened by the dust. The doctor had long since died and his descendants no longer cared about preserving their ancestral home.

A woman who chewed only with her front teeth lived across the way. It was said that she had never used her molars. My uncle Costika, the only villager who raised doves, lived farther on. Aunt Vera, the Russian, lived down below. On the other side, was a woman who worked at the corner store, where I ended up finding Daniel, hiding behind a pile of tin cans.

For the thousandth time, I wondered why everything around me seemed so tainted, irrevocably blemished. Why did I get chills up my spine, why did I feel miserable when I got close to my own past? It was as if I had committed a crime myself and was compelled to re-enact it every day. Why couldn't I admit that if things had occurred this way, I just had to grin and bear it? It wasn't my fault. It wasn't anyone's fault.

How much longer was I going to feel ashamed about our Sunday dinner, our holiday meal? It consisted of sour soup, hard-boiled eggs, a roast served with grilled tomatoes, washed down with wine which we would all drink from the same glass. I felt ashamed because I never saw my father, except at Sunday dinner, and never felt comfortable around him. Ashamed of having seen my mother, once the table had been cleared after the big noon-day meal and once everyone was taking a nap, lying stark naked in the middle of the yard in a bathtub filled with water that had been warmed by the sun. Of being awakened, the next day, Monday morning, by the head of the cooperative who was coming to give orders to my mother about where she would be working that day. In my dreams, he was telling her to pick up her spade and go weed the cornfields down by the three acacias. I felt ashamed because my mother would come home from work in the evening as exhausted as a race-horse after running, her beautiful face covered in dust, grown swarthy from exposure to the sun, after which she would make a beeline for the bucket of water and gulp down two big pitchers full without taking a breath. Ashamed because we had no fruit in winter and because food was so bland and so scarce in the spring.

Perhaps I was ashamed of having observed lambs, pigs, and chickens being slaughtered. Or of having caught my parents in the act of being amorous, because love was supposed to happen to other people and not to your parents. Or perhaps I was ashamed because I listened in on their terrible quarrels. I would sweat under the covers with my eyes closed, listening for the slaps, blows, and hollering. Doors would be slammed violently. Then I would hear the voice of my grandmother, never my grandfather, who would try to restore some kind of calm. When I heard my mother crying, I knew that we had reached the end. I would feel relieved, I would also shed a few tears, grateful that once again everything had ended well.

September

Ilie paid me a visit at the beginning of September, a few weeks before the grape harvest began. He had come back alone, by train. He had concocted a story for his wife and had run over to meet me, breathless. He came toward me lit up with the happiness of a lover, ready to continue something that hadn't even started. He looked around for Daniel, who was nowhere to be found at that time of the afternoon. Daniel would be sleeping or playing somewhere, in the house or in the garden under the shade of a tree. Because we were alone, Ilie tried to kiss me, but I stopped him, feeling intimidated by his tall stature. Now that I was so close to what I had always desired, I felt overcome by fear.

Ilie took me over to his place. The large door of the house, which I had seen padlocked, was now wide open, pushed against the wall. I was greeted by a sweet smell from inside, which was mixed with the scent of varnish. Ilie had laid out packages of fruit and cakes on a small chest, draped with a green cotton placemat. He knew exactly what I would want because the village had not changed at all. I was starved for the sinful tastes of caramel, sweet pastries covered with whipped cream, oozing in butter and artificially coloured, just like I had been as a child. Since coming back here, I had all but forgotten the taste of chocolate and pastry. I had been living in a world where there were only tomatoes and dry bread.

But now, I could smell the perfume of an orange to my heart's content. Then Ilie opened a bottle of vodka and served me a glass, which I drank in one gulp. I had suspected for a long time that I had a hidden passion for alcohol. Until this time, circumstances alone had helped me curb this potential weakness, which was etched in my genetic code.

We became slightly drunk, which allowed us to ease into lovemaking. Going to bed with Ilie was very simple, nothing like the scenarios that I had envisioned, during so many sleepless nights and idle days. He took my hand and led me into the bedroom where his parents had once slept during the winter. It was only after we undressed that I felt embarrassed at how dirty I was. I had not anticipated that things would move along at such a pace.

As I had suspected, the fact that Ilie was so tall made it hard to perform sex normally. I tried to adapt to his height, although it was very awkward, as he was trying to get to where he wanted to be as quickly as possible. A few seconds later, I saw his engorged penis, which was extremely long even before he got an erection. We rolled around in the bed once occupied by my asthmatic Aunt Cecilia. The image of my aunt as she leaned back on her cushions, shivering in the dark, haunted me as her son nibbled at my neck and chin. After the passion he aroused in me, I realized that he was very much unlike the man I had imagined. I had even believed that he never thought about his mother. He may well have breathed a sigh of relief when she passed away, but he had loved her tremendously while she was still alive. He was the kind of person who didn't remember or regret anything. The village had remained unchanged for him, and the silence all around it seemed normal. And if the inhabitants were all dead and their homes deserted, so what? He still had a vineyard and vegetable garden to look after, and he would keep doing it even if he were the only one left.

I was happy that our fling had been both spontaneous and swift. It didn't bother me that he could have made love with another woman. What mattered to me was that I had finally satisfied what had been perhaps the most vital desire of my childhood.

Ilie lay down beside me, his heart beating quickly after an extremely powerful orgasm. He wrapped his long and hairy arm around me, just above my breasts, and closed his eyes.

The bedroom we were in was just as cluttered with ugly decorations as my own house. Our mothers had made such a huge effort for nothing. Their legacy was of no value and of little use to us. Ilie's wife had not taken any items. She had left them all to rot haphazardly, to be eaten away by mice or moths. The only thing that anyone had bothered to take care of were the geraniums sitting in pots on the windowsill.

A few minutes later, Ilie opened his eyes and smiled at me. He started to stroke a geranium leaf and then touched the end of my nose with his finger, which had the strong scent of geranium on it. It was getting dark outside. I had to leave to take care of my son whereas Ilie wanted to keep me at his house at any cost. Our affair was the only thing on his agenda. He had nothing else to do here. He had come all the way from Bucharest just to see me, just for my body and the promise that it held in this place of immense solitude. I assured him that I would return as soon as my son had fallen asleep and that I would stay with him the entire night.

I found Daniel perched on the large metal gate. Ever since he had lost his way and spent an entire night in a deserted house, he didn't dare leave the yard. He was so pleased to see me again after such a long absence that he cried out. His joy made me happy, too, happy at having made love and happy because I had a child. I wrapped him in my arms and gave him several warm kisses on both cheeks.

That night, after putting Daniel to bed, I got dressed and quietly left the house. It was very dark out. I could hear the mournful hooting of an owl coming from my godmother's abandoned house. I was afraid to go out into the deserted streets alone. I sat on a small chair in front of the veranda. I don't know how long I stayed there, but it was very late when I heard the big gate squeaking. In the darkness I could make out the tall silhouette of Ilie just as he was passing the well. He had had a feeling that I wasn't going to come alone because it was such a dark night. We walked back over to his house together, holding hands, picking our way over the potholes in the bumpy road.

Ilie had already set out a bottle of vodka and a platter of bread and cheese on the small kitchen table. He then quickly removed the platter and put it aside, where I couldn't see it or smell it. Even afterward, the sharp odour of rotting cheese floated between us. There were still some cream cakes left on a piece of greasy cardboard. Ilie opened another chocolate bar and a bag of fondant candies. Even after I was full, I couldn't take my eyes off the array of treats on display, there for the taking. It was like a mirage to me. I had been deprived of treats like these throughout my childhood. At this very moment, I understood just how little benefit I had derived from the time I had spent in the city and how deeply ingrained my rural upbringing was in me. It had never occurred to me to shop for sweets or cakes to bring home. After all these years, I only occasionally ate sweets, at other people's birthday parties or if someone happened to give me some. Cakes didn't exist for me, even though I loved them. When I was a child, I would crave sweets in the spring, in particular. For entire days, I would eat practically nothing. My mother would be terribly worried and despite her questions and my grandmother's, too, I couldn't explain what I was longing for. It was only now that I understood. It was a desire for perverse combinations of aromas, for a mingling of bitter and sweet tastes, to make up for the sour and salty ones with which my mouth had been tortured all winter.

Ilie talked to me about his work, as well as his marriage. He had been working for a long time in the same vegetable greenhouse and he didn't hide the fact that he had been unfaithful to his wife. Quite often, actually. A woman from the countryside, his wife believed that this behaviour was perfectly normal for a man. He suggested that I return to Bucharest as soon as possible instead of trying to spend the winter here. Didn't I know what to expect? Had I forgotten the harsh winters? My husband's mistress was already old news. The worst was yet to come, in his view.

Ilie didn't beat about the bush. He admitted that he found me attractive. He was sorry, he said, that it had taken him so long to go to bed with me and get to know my body. Whose fault was it, he wondered? Everything could have been so simple. He could have been my first lover; he would have been so pleased it I had lost my virginity to him. But in those days, when these things could have happened so easily and so simply, leaving lasting memories, I was so naïve. Back then, he had found me somewhat cold and innocent, that is, exactly the kind of girl it was better not to be involved with. He had begun to have sex when he was very young, at the age of fourteen, going to bed with bold, simple, and robust girls, who welcomed the attentions of men with a smile on their lips. He loved women who could look you in the eye without being ashamed or shy, who flaunted their boobs, who wiggled their backsides at the boys, and who gave in easily to sexual advances. The place where we lived was so vast, there was so much space, so many secret hiding places to conduct the business of love. Hadn't I made a big mistake by waiting so long to enjoy it too?

Ilie liked me a lot. He especially liked my sexual appetite, the haste with which I had thrown myself at him. He flattered himself that he had broken down the barriers of my asceticism. He fancied himself a kind of saviour, an altruist, as it were. I was crazy about his magnanimous stance: he was offering himself to me like a feast. I could eat as much as I wanted, without any restrictions, which was amazing considering how famished I was. And as his father's son, Ilie was very appreciative of my eagerness. So, I became a perfectly willing participant in a kind of sexual therapy, which became all the more pleasurable once I was no longer haunted by the image of Aunt Cecilia stretched out among her cushions.

Once we were back in bed again, after divulging our secrets, I took great care to behave the right way. I was neither too precipitous, nor too slow or lazy. I tolerated the vulgar acts and small perversions to which Ilie subjected me, without really initiating any myself. My upbringing as a country girl prevented me from engaging in extreme forms of love games, despite my deep desires and carnal instincts. I had long since understood where the boundaries lay between sexual appetite and upbringing, mentalities, and the age-old tradition of doing things "properly." When it came to sex, women should not take the reins; they should never reveal their carnal desires, they should not ignore morals or lose interest in them, and they should not completely disclose their yearnings. They didn't have permission to indulge in limitless freedom. For us, the borders were rather tight. I loved every caress I got from Ilie and appreciated each of them with all my heart. I loved it when he held his body close to mine. The rare times when I had had sex before I was married, I had never been able to get used to having my lover prop himself up by his wrists over me as if he were doing push-ups, which allowed him to look into my eyes and read the signs of pleasure on my face. Lies would very often begin at that moment, when a man looked at a woman with the curiosity of someone who is window shopping.

Ilie was completely glued to the surface of my naked body. I ran my fingers along his long spine down to the hairy groove between his buttocks. I was helping him to understand me. We were the horse and the horse-back rider out on a long ride into the dark night.

I went home before dawn. It was cold out. The mist and pungent odour of fall were already wafting in the air. I jumped into bed, wrapped my arms around Daniel, and nestled against him under the covers. He was burning hot and smelled of milk. I slept in. Daniel got up, took a piece of bread from the cupboard, and disappeared into the vineyard.

It was Ilie who woke me in the afternoon. And, because Daniel was outside, he took me in his big arms, wrapped me up in a sheet, and began to kiss me on the lips. The scent of alcohol, pastries, and sperm from the night before suddenly flooded the roof of my mouth. Even the lengthy sleep had not neutralized these flavours entirely. My body was still tingling from intercourse and my stomach had not completed the digestive process. Ilie had come to pick me up and take me for a car ride in the countryside. Daniel jumped in with us, unconcerned about the presence of this stranger. As we drove along roads covered with three or four centimetres of dirt, the car kicked up a cloud of grey dust. We drove around sunflower and corn fields until we reached the paved road.

It suddenly occurred to Ilie that it was September 8th, the Feast of the Nativity, when the birth of the Virgin Mary is celebrated. There had always been a fair on that occasion in Radomiresti, the neighbouring village. We decided right then and there that we would go back there. It had been so much fun when we were children. I had only vague memories of the place: there was a large, fenced-in square, where a crowd would gather. At the time, I got there by a horse-drawn cart. There would be a mob of kids and we would yell all along the way. One particular memory came back to me, of being next to a merry-go-round, with a strong smell of sausages in the air. We marvelled at the stacks of watermelons and stalls piled high with tin jewellery and glass beads. I remembered the Romani people and their copper kettles.

There was a circus with a dwarf at the entrance and wild animals enclosed in wooden cages, along with heaps of candies, sesame snaps, and packets of halva. The narrow space, encircled by rickety fences, seemed infinite to me. I would spend the whole day walking around with other kids, and each time it felt new to me. My mother allowed me to take only two turns on the merry-go-round. The dizziness that came over me when the horses took off gave me an inkling, for the first time, that there was something better in the world, something beyond our poor village. That's when I began to hope and dream that I would be able to leave my own people behind forever.

Caught up in the spinning carrousel, I felt like another person. With my eyes closed and the wind in my hair, I was convinced that my life would be different. I wasn't sure what awaited me, and I didn't even know what I was hoping for. I knew even less about the way in which my life would change. But, it was going to happen one day, for sure.

My family didn't buy very much at those fairs. My mother used to shop at the village store, where the goods were better and more useful. Yet the fairs were part of my memories of the old days, with their street vendors, acrobats, trained bears romping around a campfire, fortune-tellers, and palm-readers. They had also been important events in the lives of my grandparents when they were young. My parents, on the other hand, just thought of them as passing entertainment and a mere curiosity.

The village of Radomiresti was somewhat livelier than ours, as we saw while driving down the main street. Ilie and I looked for the fairgrounds for a long time, its main feature, in my memory, being a large well. Eventually, we had to ask a woman who was pulling a stubborn goat by a long chain, almost strangling it as it tried to nibble on the branches of a small acacia. The fair was no more.

We came back from our excursion tired and starving. Ilie took Daniel back to his place and gave him some candies. One hour later, when I realized that they were not back yet, I went to join them. I found them both ensconced in front of a small television watching cartoons. Every time that he came here, Ilie would bring his TV set and place it on the hood of his car. He made me a Nescafé, which I gulped down. At that moment, I couldn't imagine anything better in the whole world.

That evening, Ilie left for Bucharest. He said he would be back in two weeks for the grape harvest, this time with his wife and brother-in-law. I was burning with desire, but I remained silent as I watched him pack his bags. I felt as if the most beautiful part of our relationship was behind us. Whatever happened, we would never again experience the same heightened tension and pleasure as we had during our last night together, a night I had been anticipating since the age of seven. If only we could have touched one another. But Daniel was there, between us, and it would have been very mean to send him back to our house alone. Ilie left me the bottle of vodka, jar of Nescafé, and bag of candies. If Daniel hadn't seen them, I would have been greedy enough to eat them by myself, secretly, but he put his hands on them and I never saw them again.

A few days after Ilie left, I found the energy to enter the large house attached to my grandparent's house, which I had not dared to enter so far. The building had two doors, both of which were locked, and I had no idea where the keys could be. I broke one of the windows and got in that way, opening the tin door from the inside. I knew locks and hinges had never been a strong part of our house. My mother would never lock the doors, except from the inside at night, more out of superstition than out of a fear of burglars. During the day, anybody could have come in, at any time. The inside latches no longer worked at all, and the doors were always wide open.

There was dust everywhere, but everything was intact. None of the things that I remembered had disappeared. What could you still expect from a world that no longer tempted thieves? It was a sign that everything was dead, totally devastated. There was nothing to steal. The four bedrooms of the house were all fully furnished. The beds and floors were covered with rough woollen fabric. On the windows, there were two rows of floor-length drapes, sheers made of nylon and then another curtain made of handwoven linen. A little piece of embroidered canvas lay on the seats of all the chairs and the thresholds were covered with tanned goatskins.

Bundles of rags that my grandmother had collected to weave into blankets were stuffed behind the tiled stoves. My mother had stashed empty bottles, shoe boxes, worn shoes, and tangled wires helter-skelter under the beds. In the last bedroom, a large walnut wardrobe with three doors still housed the last clothes my mother had worn, my father's tunic, and a few piles of books. On the top shelf, to protect them from the light, lay two felt hats, a fur cap that was shedding in a few places, and a few wall hangings. Below them, was a vase in the shape of a fish containing three plastic chrysanthemums. Dried moth larvae hung from the ceiling. The windows were stuffed with blue paper that had been dried up by the sun. I opened the windows wide and threw out the remains of this sky-coloured matter, which disintegrated as soon as I touched it.

Once again, I got the urge to work. I tied my hair up with a piece of cloth, put on a faded, old T-shirt, and, with little else for equipment, I bravely sallied forth into the dusty kingdom. It took me an entire day to clear out the old rags and chairs, boxes, and dressers, furniture I was able to move by myself. I took all the pieces of needlework or embroidery I found and ruthlessly banished them from the lifeless tomb that my house had become. I piled everything up in the middle of the yard and set the entire heap on fire. I kept only a few bedsheets that were not moth-eaten along with some cotton towels. Everything made of wool or feathers was infested with bugs: pillows, mattresses, blankets, and sweaters. Everything came apart in my hands.

The wardrobes had remained empty. In the corners, along the baseboards, you could see mouseholes, visibly stuffed with clumps of cut-up paper. I wiped the moths off the ceilings and the spider webs out of the corners. I washed the windows and hosed the walls down with water. The rooms became large and spacious, and the sun shone brightly through the windows.

Daniel was euphoric, too. He ran from one end of the house to the other, getting up on the beds and chairs and trying to climb up to the top of the stoves. He even helped me carry some of the items from my grandparents' shack to my parents' house. We were finally moving, finally getting out of our dingy hovel. We moved into the second bedroom. At the entrance, there was a small patio, the only cement surface. On the threshold, the mason had lodged a coin which I had often tried to pry out with a nail when I was young. Then there was a long and narrow room, which had served as a kitchen for a short time. Inside there was the door to the tiled stove that heated the other room, which we were going to occupy.

Our bedroom had a bed, an armchair, a table with four chairs, and a large wooden trunk where we kept the bedding. It had two windows, one looking out on the patio of the adjoining room with a view of the street. The next room was covered with a sort of awning and was connected to the other patio by means of a large swinging door. The last room was the guestroom, but you couldn't sleep there because there was a pen of very noisy geese right next to it. A very large wardrobe, now empty, was still standing in this room, along with a bed with almost all its springs broken, and a table with two padded chairs. The roof over this room obviously had a leak because there was a large black stain on the ceiling. Once the fall rains began, the plaster was sure to crumble, and water would leak into the house.

After this short inspection, I looked for a trapdoor leading to the attic. I found it in the first room. With considerable effort, I managed to climb up on two chairs placed one on top of the other and open the heavy door. Daniel wanted desperately to go with me, and he finally convinced me with a flood of bitter tears. The attic extended over the entire surface of the house. Next to the tall chimney, I saw two large clay pots in which my grandmother stored grease to make soap with. At the other end, there was still a pile of wheat, full of mouse droppings. On the blackened rafters there were a few empty wasp nests. The tiles were still in good condition. The wind had blown only a few tiles off the part of the roof that faced the street. I decided that I would make it a priority to put some pots or basins under the holes in the roof before the fall storms started.

I went back down and, for the fun of it, I pretended to leave Daniel behind in the attic. His tears and cries of fright quickly put an end to my prank. We soon made up and once again inspected the house together. I began with the kitchen, which was cluttered with furniture. I didn't know what to do to restore the room to its initial purpose. I could already picture myself comfortably settled in, making cakes for the winter. I didn't care if there was no oven and if the hearth had been destroyed. My mother had furnished it with an antique Récamier loveseat and an armoire with double doors. This made the room look quite narrow, like a railway car loaded with freight. All the rooms had become bedrooms in a way. The entire house was like a display window: full of beautiful but completely useless objects. Each room had a bed, a wardrobe, a table, and set of chairs. There was no trace of a kitchen or bathroom. I tried to move the wooden armoire out, but it was too heavy. I was disappointed and didn't even try to move the bed, which I would obviously not have the strength to do. I might have been able to dismantle the bed first, and then move the pieces into another room. But instead, I opted for another solution. I pinned all my hopes on Ilie.

With this move, we were farther from the outhouse, located way back beyond the edge of the yard. When we first came here, even Daniel went there. Then, when we began to find it a bit too far, we decided we would only go there for "number two." To have a pee, I chose a little spot behind my grandparents' shack, whereas Daniel would urinate anytime and anywhere he wanted to, even in the front yard. For the first few months, I didn't worry about it, but once the summer heatwaves arrived, the stench became unbearable. And so I made him go in the garden near the vineyard. I had to spare the hole in the outhouse because it wasn't deep and looked like it might fill up more quickly than expected. I had to be economical because I was not at all capable of digging another one. Green flies buzzed over the pile of fecal matter beneath the hole.

Daniel carved out a space for himself in the new house. He brought in all his toys from outside, toys that were our only link to the civilized world, to which he added a pile of rusty tin cans that he had found buried in the yard. The entire house, in fact, became his property. He roamed freely from room to room. We had placed everything that he was able to gather from outdoors on the floors. Daniel now refused to leave the house. Through the wide-open windows I could hear him talking out loud all day long, getting into arguments with his lead soldiers.

I delighted in the last rays of summer sun. In the middle of the yard, I had placed a thick sheet on which I lay stretched out most of the day. Lying on my stomach during this time, I merely scratched the surface of the layer of dust. If the sun was cloud-covered, I turned my face toward it and spent hours watching the white masses drift by overhead. Sailing with the clouds, I forgot all about my surroundings. The rays of sunshine that occasionally broke through the cloud cover pinned me to the ground. I would wake up with my bones piercing my flesh, my kidneys burning, and my bladder swollen.

The yard was full of leaves. The acacias had long since been denuded. They were the first to turn green in the spring, but also the first to rush into hibernation.

The second pear tree, the surviving brother of the one that was planted next to the oven, had also shed most of its greenery. The quince trees, on the other hand, still had their waxy leaves, which seemed even more abundant once they had been cruelly deprived of their fruit. They had been like this forever. The trees in our garden were good for nothing except providing shade. Their fruits were small, shrivelled up, and full of worms. But no one dared to cut the trees down. They were left to die a natural death, like people. They were not replaced until their trunks had rotted from old age.

I routinely postponed the task of sweeping up the leaves and burning them. I waited for them to pile up even more. The only good thing I had managed to do since coming here was to grow a few tomato plants. Despite my pessimism, they had proved to be unexpectedly productive. I had been so inept, ignorant actually, about the life cycle of plants that I thought they were sterile at the beginning. Now all the tendrils were full of fat, fleshy tomatoes, even though I had supported them with just a few stakes. They were intertwined, overlapping to protect their fruit from getting spoiled if they touched the ground. I felt secure with this basic food and didn't dare to think about what was going to happen. I still refused to think seriously about whether I wanted to stay here for the winter, or whether I could even do so. How would I heat the house and what was I going to eat for six months?

I could now see that I was living in a civilized world, although without civilization. That I was having more trouble surviving here than Robinson Crusoe on his desert island! That it would have been ten times better to have been shipwrecked! I realized that it was always better to start over from scratch than to try to make up for a bad beginning.

One day, I was looking at the immense tiled stove in our bedroom. There was no longer a chimney and the bricks inside were crumbling. I couldn't repair it or use it, and, above all, I had nothing to burn in it. So, I would have liked to make it disappear. I had a strange desire for space. All I dreamed about was extending my space. I wanted to get rid of everything so I could see the true size of my bedroom. This act of deconstruction, I felt, would set me free. Something was still weighing on me. The heavy, compact stove made me feel powerless. I wondered how I could demolish it. Where was I to start? Should I begin by breaking the lid and then taking it apart brick by brick? But where would I find a hatchet or a hammer?

That was the last time I wanted to change or adapt something. I finally resigned myself to the situation. There was nothing to be done. I just had to live, to the extent possible, with this disastrous legacy. Nothing could be fixed or altered in any way. I had tried, without success, to free the yard of its ugly and useless buildings, but there was no one left to remove the broken-down oven, the dried-up well, the barren trees, the fence that was trying to stand up to the invading briar, the cement that covered the earth and prevented wildflowers from seeding. Nothing could be done except wait patiently for natural devastation. The Robinson model was turning out to be of no use to me. I could not organize the matter that surrounded me for the simple reason that it needed to be destroyed rather than organized. I would not really be set free until matter stopped taking the place of people.

Then I heard Ilie's car. In the deep silence surrounding the house, the least bit of noise had the explosive power of an atomic bomb. He was coming for the grape harvest, accompanied by his wife and brother-in-law.

What useless work he was doing! The small quantity of wine that Ilie was able to produce was equivalent to only a quarter of the time and effort spent on the process. But how could you object to it? In former times, would you have been able to convince your parents that their work was of no use? Our ancestors were involved in activities that were just as unprofitable and badly remunerated, which they had inherited from their forebears, of whom they were nonetheless justifiably proud. They had neither the power nor the desire to change anything whatsoever or to think about it in any other way. Who would have been able to convince Ilie to make better use of his money or leisure time? For our parents, the problem was not to capitalize on their work, or to make it more lucrative, but to survive to the extent possible.

This time, Ilie introduced me to his brother-in-law and his wife, Petruta. She looked like a gentle and docile person, despite her rapacious gaze. But she seemed nervous about any woman in her husband's presence. The brother-in-law bowed, took my hand, and put it to his lips. The way in which he squeezed my fingers left no doubt as to his what was going on in his mind. Especially since Ilie had announced jokingly that I had been living here all alone since the spring.

I offered to help them, and they were happy to accept, except for Petruta, who didn't want me to put myself out. Ilie had everything he needed for the grape harvest: a large wooden tub in which they would press the grapes, and pipes for fermenting the grape must.

The barrels had been cleaned the preceding year when the entire grape harvest had been ruined by very early rains. Now, he just had to leave them for a day to soak and swell in a mixture of boiling water, absinthe, and walnut tree leaves.

We, the women, picked the grapes, filling large baskets that Petruta's brother carried back to the tub. Ilie stomped on the grapes. The must flowed drop by drop into a large cauldron, which was covered with gauze to filter the few seeds that might have worked their way in. As soon as the cauldron was full, the brother-in-law would carry the must to the barrels in the cellar. The first day, we harvested grapes from the vines along the house and, the next day, we took care of the slightly smaller ones, which were planted outside the village. After we were finished, we shook a walnut tree, which had grown randomly beside the little stream bordering Ilie's property. All this activity now seemed like nothing more than a brief summer distraction.

When there was no wine, the winters were terrible in these places tormented by the wind. The years when phylloxera attacked the fruit, when summers were too dry, or when autumns were too wet, were years of grieving. The sadness of the outdoors penetrated the souls and faces of the people. Food no longer had any taste, and festivities without drunkenness lost all their beauty.

Ilie was as happy as a clam with the few buckets of wine he was going to get. He poured the must into two barrels and then assembled a rudimentary system for channelling the fermentation residue that was going to flow into the cauldron.

I was quite familiar with this process. I would have been able to do many things if I had had the strength.

My very practical nature, the very realistic way I looked at the world, had always prevented me from letting loose. Now I had lost that natural peasant instinct, that down-to-earth vision of existence and its necessities. When I lived in the city, Mihai had many times been astonished by my overly frugal way of organizing my affairs. I was a good cook, but I didn't waste my time in the kitchen. I went shopping when I had very little money in my pocket. I avoided spending money on anything that wasn't immediately useful. I was adept at sewing, mending, alterations, and knitting. My peasant great-grandmothers had taught me all those useless skills, and several others that I could add to my repertoire. My life consisted of performing a few actions and repeating them forever. All that was required of me was to be born, to live, and to die like an ant. That was it, my extraordinary destiny!

In the evening, when we had finished working, we celebrated the grape harvest. Ilie's wife looked at me, with a smile but also intense curiosity. Whenever I looked in her direction, I caught her staring at me. She seemed especially judgmental because I was drinking with the men while she barely touched a drop of alcohol. She was the only one who cooked the meat and cleared the dishes. Daniel complained of a stomachache after drinking too much must.

There were fewer mosquitoes and flies. When people were dying, these nightmarish insects proliferated, even in the absence of human beings. Fall had always been a short season, one that made us happy; during the few weeks at the beginning of the season, we enjoyed beautiful sunsets and the summer heat that lingered on, without causing our skin to blister.

Ilie was going to stay in the village for a few days, until the end of the fermentation process, which he needed to monitor closely. Petruta had not reacted to this piece of news. The next day, I learned that she had decided to leave without her brother.

The following night, Ilie came to get me at my house. He tapped lightly on the window that opened onto the cement path. I took him into my grandparents' bedroom where I had made the bed the day before. This time, my memories were poisoned. I couldn't help thinking about my grandfather's brown face, which stared down at me from a photograph; I was haunted by the pallid face of my grandmother the night before she died, and the commotion at her funeral. All manner of petty, trivial, and insignificant things came to mind while Ilie, on top of me with his back arched, penetrated me and sucked my tongue to the same rhythm. He didn't notice how detached and distracted I was, not participating, even formally, in his love game. Ilie was self-sufficient. The thought of cheating on his wife, the symbol of eternal marriage, was enough for him to find making love with me marvellous. He didn't care very much whether he gave me pleasure or whether I was truly immersed in it.

He resisted sleep stubbornly. While he was tired after the strenuous days of work, he didn't want to fall asleep. He wanted to talk to me and then make love all over again, until we were just as exhausted as we had been the first night we spent together. I couldn't tell him anything about myself, however. I had almost lost the habit and art of speaking. I didn't know where or how to begin. He, on the other hand, was as inexhaustible as his mother. He had even clung to memories of the time he spent in the army, which he told me about in excruciating detail.

After a while, I absorbed his stories like the hum of a distant radio.

Lying by Ilie's side, I was swept away by a frenzied and endless dream. I dreamed that I was a child again, waiting with my mother for the floodwaters to recede. The village was totally inundated, except for a few shacks built into the hillside. We were both on the roof, sitting on sacks of wool that my mother had been able to save, with our two ducks and the rooster by our side. My father was dressed in his army uniform, and my grandparents were waving to us from another rooftop. The water had risen to the middle of the yard. Some pieces of wood were floating on the surface. No, they were rats. In the house, beetles were coming in through the chimney.

Then it was summer. On the banks of the dried-up river bed, snails floated on the surface of a mud puddle. A cricket fell out of the branches of the apple tree and landed in my hair. My grandfather was deathly ill. He stayed in the yard all day, lying on a wooden bench, covered with an old torn coat. I heard him ask what time we were eating. But the others had refused to give him food, because they couldn't put a stop to his diarrhea.

It smelled like fire.

My mother was hiding a bottle of *tuica* under the table. She was the only one who took pity on the old man. He had given her the right to poison him slowly with the plum brandy. Every night, my grandmother changed my grandfather's underpants the way she would have changed a baby. She was always surprised that his bodily fluids didn't stop, despite the Black Fast that had been imposed on him. Because he smelled so bad, he was not allowed to sit down with us at the table. My father wanted to make another bed for him, but my grandmother was always against the idea. My mother gave him liquor to drink surreptitiously, once everyone had gone to bed. At night, my grandfather was in unbearable pain. He would go into the vineyard and howl like a wolf.

I was once again on the floating roof, watching my grandmother standing in the middle of the road, her legs numb. She was up to her knees in mud.

I could smell the aroma of bread. And then I could smell cheese, which was hanging in a corner to drain, covered on all sides with green flies.

I loved the meal they used to serve after burying the dead. As children, we would gather around a table laden with *colaci*, sweet buns which, according to Orthodox custom, would ensure that the deceased were fed in the afterlife. My grandmother would light candles inserted into each of the golden loaves while my mother put chunks of white squash out on a glass platter. We waited for my grandfather to be buried before eating the *colaci* made for him. If one of the candles went out, it was a sign that the old man had tasted the food.

One winter, all the crosses in the cemetery disappeared. The villagers had taken them and divided them up among themselves to fuel their fires until spring came.

The smell of cheese still lingered in the air.

Ilie was still sleeping beside me with his hands under his head. I pulled the sheet up over him. Something had bitten me on the arm and left an enormous welt. Fleas! They had made my life miserable when I was a child. I nervously scratched the itchy bite. Then I discovered another, above my right knee. And another one on my shoulder. I got up, grabbed my shirt, and went into the other house. Daniel was sleeping, as usual, with no covers on. The sheets were all bunched up at the foot of the bed. I lay down next to him and fell asleep right away.

When he left, Ilie did not wake me. He came back the next day around noon, this time by car, to go for a ride. We took off quickly so that Daniel wouldn't see us.

Ilie and I stopped the car far from the village, at the edge of a cornfield. He put the front seat of the car down and took off his pants. I pulled my skirt up. I was naked underneath. He tried to get on top of me, but his feet didn't have any support while mine were resting on the dashboard. The gear shift was poking into my left hip. We were screwing and laughing at the same time. Then I changed position. I got on top of him and wrapped my legs around his waist.

Then we went to another spot, farther along. All I had to do was glance at him and he would stop the car in the middle of the road. We weren't particularly careful because, where we were, we could see anyone coming toward us for at least a kilometre. Anyone who might have prevented us from making love was dead. The surrounding silence had been specially orchestrated so that we could hear our own grunts and moans. We could make love in only one position: Ilie lying flat on the driver's seat and me on top, pressing the sole of my left foot against the stick shift. But by repeating the exercise, we discovered that moving over by just one centimetre, either forward or backward, could change everything, increase our pleasure, and make it deeper, more secret.

Because of the intense heat, Ilie had opened all the windows. We were like two wind-up dolls in a music box.

From time to time, gusts of wind would blanket us in a cloud of dust, mixed with straw and fragments of corn husks. But nothing could stop us anymore.

In the evening, Ilie took me to his place. The brother-in-law was waiting for us, with the table set. He had been drinking alone, but he wasn't so drunk that he made jokes about us. When given a discreet signal, he left, and I pounced on Ilie. I put my arms around his neck and began to kiss him all over his face. The brother-in-law's presence had made me feel ill at ease and had driven me to the brink of despair. I was going to spend the winter alone, without Ilie, without the warmth of the sun. I was going to go crazy without him and he wouldn't even know about it. Ilie didn't understand anything. He was born to make love. He wasn't interested in anything else.

We made love for a long time, with our clothes on, on the edge of the bed. Sometimes, Ilie would stop me, for just a second, before ejaculating. I would remain still in his arms, waiting for the burning fluid to recede into the tissues of his body.

When he was leaving, Ilie gave me the key to his cellar. He didn't know when or how he would be able to come and see me. He was sure that his wife would be more suspicious from now on and that she would not let him go away alone. I could take as much wine as I liked and anything else from the house I needed.

That was how we parted and that was how the month of September came to an end.

October

In October the rains began, earlier than usual. Since arriving here, I hadn't yet seen any real rain. I had long since forgotten how the rain smelled, how it sounded, what colour it was. Then the weather took a turn for the worse. For two weeks, the cold and wind kept us shut in the house, wrapped in blankets. If the wind blew from the southwest, a tiny trickle of water leaked under the windows, which could no longer be shut tight. I couldn't eat anymore. I scarcely chewed anything, except when I reluctantly gnawed on a piece of dry bread. I didn't wash up either and I went to the bathroom in a bucket which I emptied at night.

It rained all day. The trees had kept a few yellowed leaves at the very top, with a few withered and blackened fruits that had not dropped off during the summer. The briar in the garden was dried up. There were only a few thin branches left. The rosebush was the only shrub that still had green leaves on it. The roses had also disappeared earlier than usual this year. Nothing seemed to want to fight for survival, everything was overcome by a drive to vanish as quickly as possible, to begin the long sleep of winter.

It was cold out, and so cold in our bedroom. I had stomach cramps and Daniel once again had a cold, quite a serious one this time. I didn't let him get out of bed. He coughed constantly and his upper lip was always covered with a thick coat of mucus. Despite this, he insisted on getting up and walking about the cold and empty rooms of the house.

One Friday, when it was a bit milder, I got dressed in all my summer clothes and went to Aunt Joana's house to pick up our bread. I found her hanging the washing out in the yard, dressed in a thin blouse. I stayed at her house for several hours, seated next to a hot stove where she was boiling a large pot of water. In one corner of the kitchen, my aunt had prepared her weekly bath in a big wooden tub, which was lined with a thin layer of galvanized tin. The room smelled of liquid soap blended with the scent of rainwater, which had been collected in barrels and stored under the awning. Women loved this combination. The laundry came out so clean after being washed in rainwater, with liquid soap made from grease and caustic soda. My aunt was boiling kernels of corn in a clay pot. On the table, there were a few dried morsels of beets that had been roasted over the fire.

As I was leaving, she gave me a few aspirin tablets, rather surprised that I had caught a cold when the weather was so nice. She hadn't yet lit the fire in her bedroom and didn't intend to do so until November. But I was a "lady," as she said, I had become used to heated apartments, to the good life. She took a piece of newspaper and wrapped up some pieces of cooked duck for Daniel. She didn't have any cheese, and wouldn't have any more until spring because the goats were pregnant. Again, she expressed surprise at my aversion to cheese.

I kept the small amount of money I had left in my pocket. From my aunt's house, I took a side road, passing a few piles of trash before getting to the store in the village centre. The storekeeper looked at me closely.

He was called Dinut and had been a classmate of mine in high school. Back then, he had been a chubby little boy who sat at the desk behind mine. I almost never spoke to him. When I went into his dark and narrow shop, he was cleaning the floor with diesel fuel. He let me take a leisurely look at his amply stocked shelves while he slowly continued his chores. He was dipping a brush with long bristles into a bucket of the black liquid, the surface of which looked like an iridescent metallic mirror.

Dinut didn't say a word to me, and I didn't speak to him either. I stayed there just to warm up because the store had an electric heater. I was as pathetic as a drowned rat. Dinut had on a thick woollen sweater and a fur cap while I was barefoot and dressed in a couple of faded T-shirts.

I asked him whether he had any antibiotics. No, he did not. Here people were not used to buying medication. Sometimes they would die from a mere flu only because medicine was too abstract for them. You only went to a doctor if you had very bad luck. I went home again absolutely frozen. Daniel was playing with his tin cans on the bare floor and was coughing his guts out. I gave him a spanking and packed him off to bed. We both took an aspirin and went to sleep.

I then fell into a state of lethargy. I no longer knew when the day began and when night ended. I emptied the bucket of urine mechanically and showed Daniel that there was bread on the table. To force him to stay in bed, I allowed him to bring all his toys with him. He had put dirty cans on the covers and then, when he saw that I was always asleep, he had added structures he had made from corncobs.

One morning, I realized, with horror, that I was pregnant. I tried to get out of bed and suddenly felt so nauseous that I collapsed, my stomach churning. There was no doubt. I was pregnant! I stayed in bed till the afternoon. I wanted to postpone any further confirmation. I only went out when I felt that my bladder was about to explode. I was mainly afraid of the odour of the bucket that awaited me on the veranda. And I was right. As soon as I opened the door, I began to barf. I wasn't even able to do it over the bucket, in fact, and I didn't want to. I knew that I would have passed out if I had smelled its putrid contents.

Daniel was crying behind me. He was asking me if I was going to die. I pushed him back into the house so that he wouldn't see the greenish liquid I had vomited onto the floor. I cleaned it up with a rag, and then I went outside to get some air.

I felt hot and cold at the same time. I no longer felt the drops of water falling on my naked toes. I had the feeling that there was a ring of fire around my pelvis, crackling as it came into contact with the rain and wind. I huddled up against the veranda wall and broke into tears.

I would have to pay again! I had never been forgiven for the least bit of foolishness, the slightest misstep. There were so many criminals on the loose. And what had I done compared to them? I was nothing but an insignificant petty thief. I was going to be punished without mercy. Why would I never be granted pardon?

Daniel had heard me sobbing and had come out in his bare feet to see me. He was crying as loud as I was and begged me not to die, not to leave him alone. He was shaking like a leaf, but he didn't move away. I wanted to hug him, but the smell of urine and the pungent odour of his clothes, which hadn't been washed for a month, made me nauseous again. I had just enough time to push him away and move a little farther off before having another terrible bout of vomiting. Daniel would not stop crying. Between two heaves, I yelled at him to stop whining. But when he heard my raspy voice, he cried even harder.

When I stopped vomiting, he stopped crying. I stayed crouched over, my chin on my knees. Daniel was shaking my shoulder. The two of us were soaked to the bone. As if we had wept with every fibre of our being.

"It's nothing, it's not serious, go back in the house," I said to him repeatedly. But he was holding on to me. He had wrapped his skinny arms around my neck and would not let go.

I had trouble getting up and tottered as I walked. I wiped my eyes. I took Daniel by the hand and led him back into the house.

He had lost interest in his games. He watched me all day while I remained in bed, motionless, lying on my back with my eyes open, staring at the ceiling. He didn't eat all day and I didn't say anything about it. In the evening, he came to lie down next to me. Once again, he put his arms around my neck and pressed up against my body.

After that, I no longer kept track of what he was doing all day. In the darkness, I sometimes felt him at my side. I no longer heard him when he got in and out of bed. Sometimes, he would try to wake me up and get me to eat. He would hand me a piece of dry and mouldy bread. I would ask him to bring me a little water. There was none left. He was also thirsty. For days, he had only been drinking the rainwater stagnating under the awning. The water was dirty, but he lapped it up without worrying about it. He also brought me some, in a rusty tin that he was using as a glass. The water tasted of minerals, of all the salts in the earth, and sank to the bottom of my stomach like alcohol. The mouthful I drank upset my stomach and made my anesthetized body ache again.

I tried, one last time, to reach the well. I leaned against the wooden fence as I walked, trying to lift my feet out of the thick mud that covered the ground. My shoes were soaking and my legs were wet up to my knees. All my efforts were for naught. I was so weak that I could not turn the immense iron wheel of the well. I tried to pull the wooden bucket up from the bottom of the black hole. I looked despondently at the still mirror deep inside, which reflected the contours of my head looking like a dark little stain on the water. Everything was hopeless! I would never manage, just as I would never warm up again. It was cold, very cold, always so cold! The world was plunged into a terrible cold.

So, because I couldn't get the well to work, I had to quench my thirst with rainwater, which Daniel filtered through a handkerchief. The only thing that I sometimes told him to do was to eat.

"You should eat. Bread. Go eat some bread."

And then I would fall asleep again.

One day, I was awakened by a strange humming sound. It felt like it was the middle of summer, and I was outside, lying under the apple tree watching a swarm of bees.

When I opened my eyes, there was a young man sitting on the edge of my bed. He was bent over me and was shaking me. I looked at him intently, but I absolutely didn't recognize him. His head was rather big, and his eyes were close to his nose. He was speaking. He was speaking to me. Daniel was nearby and was pulling my hand.

As he shook me, the young man sat me up. It was Mihai. I didn't understand what he was asking me to do, but I had finally recognized him. He continued to shake me. Then I slowly began to make out the last words he had uttered.

"Speak to me, say something!"

He was so violent that Daniel was frightened. He came close to me in the bed and hung on to me for dear life.

I would have liked to answer Mihai or at least understand what he was saying to me. I was not able to do so. Finally, I came up with some basic expressions.

"Is it still raining out?"

He had stopped shaking me, convinced at last that I was not dead. He held out a piece of chocolate for me. I took it and looked at it for a long time. It looked like a clump of mud, like the ones left in the riverbed during the summer drought. I handed it to Daniel. But he had already eaten some of it. He still had a faint brown mustache around his lips from the chocolate. He took it anyway and popped it in his mouth. Mihai was looking at me. I didn't want to worry him, I didn't need to have him fuss over me. I was starting to wake up and said,

"I don't need anything."

Daniel, on the contrary, was ravenous. He sat down at the table, where Mihai had put out some packages he had unwrapped, and began to eat. They left me alone for a minute. I immediately fell asleep again, huddled up against the wall.

I felt myself being shaken again. Mihai had his face close to mine and was saying something to me. I could smell his breath.

"I don't understand. I don't understand anything," I was telling him. "Leave me alone!"

And I fell asleep again.

When I woke up, there was a deathly silence around me. I opened my eyes. The room was empty and dark. And cold. It was so cold! I couldn't keep warm anymore. I didn't understand why.

I opened my eyes again and, this time, saw a dazzling light. On the table there was a white parcel. But I didn't see Daniel. Something was whispering. The sun perhaps.

Rays of light were shining on the surface of the deeply embedded ceramic tiles. Their diagonal placement was mesmerizing. Looked at from another angle, they were lined up vertically, as well as horizontally.

Why had the door remained open? I usually closed it, and held it shut with a chair. That's why it was so cold. I smelled vanilla and then got a whiff of caramel.

How cold it was. Cold! Cold!

I was dreaming about the stork's nest at the top of the acacia planted near the fence separating our property from my godmother's. At the back of her house, a wall was covered with rows of eggshells. I had once hidden in that house with Stela and Manole. Beyond the fences, children chased us and threw stones at us. Manole went from her to me. Stela didn't want to have sex with him anymore, because he had hurt her. But I wanted to keep going. It had also hurt me, but I wanted to go all the way, once and for all.

I was afraid of my father. When I saw him in the distance, coming home on the main road, I would hide so that he wouldn't see me.

Stela liked to tear earthworms apart. After the heavy rains of autumn, the streets would be full of worms. Like Daniel, she would hold one end in each hand and then pull until the worm broke in two. I didn't like that.

Instead, I liked to do experiments with eyes, with the little piece of retina that I would detach from the lens. I would take the eye of a dead chicken and puncture it with a nail. A whitish liquid would flow out of the cavity. I would wait for my father to kill the rabbit kept in a cage on the patio. I would try to grab the rabbit's head before my mother got a chance to throw it into a pot of boiling water. But I didn't touch the lambs. Their eyes were too big and too scared looking. I remembered little Alba, slaughtered two days before Easter. The only thing left of her was her bloody muzzle, the tips of her ears, and her hooves.

Flies were buzzing around the dripping cheese. I want to throw up!

I went to the cemetery with my grandmother to weed the patch of land around my grandfather's grave. With my fingernails, I scraped the wax that had gathered around the base of the cross so that my grandmother could light more candles. She asked my grandfather aloud whether he wanted to smoke.

Outside, night had fallen. I believe there was a full moon that night. A sliver of light penetrated the inside of the house, lighting up the ceramic tiles. I had the feeling that someone was looking through the window, staring at me. I was terribly cold, even though I had not totally lost the heat and light of the candles that my grandmother had lit.

Looking up at the ceiling, I went back over the discussions I used to have with Ileana in Bucharest, while she was trimming green beans or peeling potatoes. When I talked to her about my parents, she would always find something to do in the kitchen so that she wouldn't waste time.

Was it possible that there was another world somewhere, where grandmothers had brothers who were as good-looking as the ones my grandmother had? Where there were blind people, one-armed people, men and women? Where people would grow tomatoes? Where there would be bottles with rusty bottlecaps? We are all so eager to talk about ourselves. Look at me, Ileana! It's possible that I will die tomorrow, and I can't accept the idea of being so insignificant. An entire world will disappear with me, a world that has existed in a certain way, but which I have understood in a completely different manner. But no matter which way I have looked at it, it really did exist. Aunt Polina, my forgotten Aunt Polina who treated my lower back pain, understood that, and that's why she cried so much at her husband's funeral. In a flash of insight, she saw that her granddaughter, Danielle, would never be acquainted with my grandmother's handsome brothers or know about the adventures of my grandfather when he was young, and that nobody would even care. That's what you would want to discover one day: a past that was like a mirror in which you could see your own reflection.

One night, I even saw Calin, a clumsy Roma minstrel who made beautiful music on his old fiddle. Every time my grandmother wanted to entertain me, she told me stories about him. And now, there he was standing in the middle of my room, at my bedside, with a violin in his hands. He looked at me and smiled so that I could see the only tooth he had left in his mouth, which was capped with a gold crown. As usual, his costume was too short and too tight, with a torn pocket that revealed a dirty handkerchief.

The villagers would call upon him on every possible occasion. The old man was a bit flabby and quite deaf. He would stand in the middle of the room, as he was doing now, and slowly begin to play the instrument he had inherited from his minstrel ancestors. No one would know what trickery he was cooking up, but my grandmother told me that he used to let out a lot of farts. That's why my grandmother was trying to play the violin a few hours before she died, when her hands were already cold.

It was so cold in the house! I thought it was daytime, whereas, fifteen minutes later, it would be dark.

Ileana had asked me one day if the people here believed in God. The real answer was that they loved God without actually believing in him very much. My grandmother didn't go to mass anymore, my grandfather swore and drank like all the other men, and my mother probably had a lover. They lived naturally, without asking any questions. What was good and what was evil? I think that these questions were only on their minds while they were fasting. My grandmother couldn't fast anymore because she was a diabetic, my father could not do without cheese, and my mother didn't like picking dandelions. They could have been punished for this. Although God was also understanding! He continued to exist even if they were not ascetic. Their God was a rather kindly and tender father who only rarely disturbed their lives. Sometimes he came closer than he needed to. God was the object of their need to love. It was not sufficient to venerate one hand. Their God had soles on his feet and even a rear end, all of which were respectable enough to be mentioned in their prayers. When they sought forgiveness, they would kiss the delicate parts of his divine body. They rebelled less and less frequently, and became resigned to the consolation offered by religion. If God wanted it to be this way, there was nothing more to do. Those were the only moral principles to follow.

But as far as my grandmother was concerned, she had been wronged. She had the misfortune to live in a vineyard, surrounded by grapes she couldn't taste because of her diabetes. The worst thing was that she had been deprived of the joy of eating bread. God had condemned her to eat polenta forever more, and her skin had been covered in the sores of pellagra since childhood. What could it mean, the fact that she had died so quickly? Had God felt remorse at the last minute? What could have been going through her mind during her last three days of suffering and farewells? Maybe she was thinking about a springtime of sweet-smelling flowers, or perhaps Calin?

One thing was certain. For them, death was the best holiday. The ritual that took place without hesitation gave them a divine role. It was the only time that God looked at them all at once, an event that never happened anywhere else.

As she was peeling carrots, Ileana was saying that there was nothing unusual about serving a dying person, about doing them one last favour. There was always someone who loved the person who was going to leave us more than all the others. Then, we were talking about my grandfather. I could still hear her speaking in a loud voice.

"It's inexcusable that your family kept him at home, with dysentery, instead of putting him in the hospital," she said. "But if that's how they did it, then nothing else mattered. Just helping him die with dignity, like a human being rather than an animal."

"What happened to our grandparents is not fair, Ileana."

"Why? I would also like to die like your grandfather. I would like to have someone near me to do me one last favour, even if it were bad for my health. It was just a matter of chance that Petre was your grandfather and not the king of Spain."

I was trying to explain to Ileana why it was so strange that Lanku's wife had left home, that she had split the house in half like a skull, and demanded the half to which she was legally entitled. How brave it was to test the world when she was so naïve! She no longer wanted to live the life to which she was destined, the way animals do. Only my mother had been foolish enough to believe that because her life had begun one way, it couldn't end any differently. Ah! Why hadn't she seen the truth in time?

You cannot convince me that a woman who wants to be happy is miserable. In any case, this empty house, abandoned like a skeleton, was proof that the unexpected had happened, in a space where nothing had happened, at least not for several centuries.

You will never be able to understand me, my dear Ileana. You will never grasp the meaning of my words. Unfortunately, no one will understand my stories! And, after me, after I disappear, no one will be able to repeat them. This place will remain as smooth as a baby's bum, as if nothing had ever existed. But who would find this a cause for concern?

In a split second of absolute clarity, everything shifted. It wasn't Calin the minstrel, nor the dreams of the flood, nor my grandparents who had invaded my bedroom.

Rays of sunlight illuminated maps of the Middle Ages hanging on the wall facing me. The room was suddenly filled with astrolabes and tables laden with baroque fruits. Caravaggio's Bacchus clasped a wine goblet with three fingers. Translucent fruit filtered the light. A few drops of juice were about to squirt out of Flemish limes and tickle my mouth. A diminutive Chinese man was seated at a small mahogany table, his feet crossed, contemplating his calligraphy brushes and inkwell. On his face was a look of exaltation, like the Buddha.

Daniel had built an entire world out of tin cans and corncobs. It was probably the last exercise in dignity, in a humble, deserted universe stretched out on the edge of an empty well.

We were poor in the land of cheese.

This time I was not sleeping. I was looking out the window at the cloudy sky. The naked branches of the apple tree sometimes tapped against the dirty windowpane. But I was still listening to Ileana who was reacting to what I had told her about the people here. To annoy me, she was telling me that she had a lot of admiration for the neighbour across the road, who was the most violent man I had ever known. She liked him because everyone else hated him, and he had the courage to challenge everyone. That man, whom she admired so much, disturbed me every night by shouting as he drove his immense flock of sheep back from the pasture. I would listen to him swearing, with my heart thumping. Every day, I wondered what he would come up with next. He hated people who were lazy. He resented them because he kept on working, even at times when other people were asleep. And that didn't make him any richer.

As night fell, I awoke and looked at the photo of my father, taped to the opposite wall under a paper icon depicting the Last Supper. I had always given as little thought as possible to this man, as far back as I could remember. I didn't want to admit how much I resembled him. Hiding behind the sober exterior was such a pathetic man. How small my mouth was and how thin my hair was, just like his. It took me a long time to get rid of the few objects that were in my way and over which I continued to stumble. I awoke violently. It was like giving birth painfully. I was hurting others because of my own weaknesses. I had not formed very strong bonds with my own child. I was so much like my father!

I couldn't remember if I had spoken to Ileana about my grandmother. Mihai said that I looked so much like her. That might have been a compliment if other people had also told me so.

In any case, when could Mihai have had a chance to get to know my grandmother? Besides, they didn't like each other. That's what I realized now. My grandmother couldn't love Mihai and he couldn't love her either.

My grandmother would often tell me about her mother, my great-grandmother Marie, the most beautiful woman in the village. She would also talk about my great-grandfather, Petre, who had had such a hard time getting Marie to marry him.

Because of herd mentality, we never disown our parents, even if they do stupid or bad things, even if they always have bad judgment. That's how I looked at those relationships, and that's the way my ancestors saw it. A direct descendant of matriarchs, Marie was like them.

In my dark dreams, Mihai did nothing but accuse me of all kinds of things, as he always had.

"Your boundless pride is the fault of your grandmother," he would tell me.

Mihai was a weak man and that's why he didn't like my grandmother. Perhaps he was afraid of her. I, too, was afraid of her. She had never been able to accept my flaws. No, Ileana, look, I am going to cry. Because I gave everything up, and my grandmother is dead.

My grandmother didn't know how to tell stories. In any case, she told only her own stories, about which she was overly passionate. Every time she revealed something to me, it was for the wrong reason. She used me to get back at everyone she had a grudge against.

I had always tried to impress my grandmother. I was continuously showing off my best side, in a perpetual attempt to move her, to get her to love me.

Again, I could hear Mihai say,

"You are only interested in impressing yourselves. I have never met women like you, who think more about themselves than about others."

In her later years, my grandmother had told me about her brothers, the most handsome men who ever lived: Nika, Radu and Bilus. In particular, she had told me—a thousand times—the story of her mother, with whom her father was madly in love, so much so that he almost killed her. Aunt Cecilia had told me the rest, but I don't blame my grandmother at all for what she had hidden from me. As far as these stories were concerned, Cecilia was more reliable, although she sometimes told lies.

It was sundown, which frightened me because at night it was always colder. I could hear my husband scolding me once again.

"There's no point in bragging about the fact that your grandmother didn't have a lover, that she never betrayed the family. In her case, as in yours, it was not a good quality. You are incapable of love until you acknowledge that you are in love. No one can be happy with you."

Only once had he been interested in something else.

"How did she die?" he had asked me when we were getting ready for bed in our apartment in Rahova.

I didn't want to talk to him about it. Because the person who had died in front of me, in front of the family and almost the entire village, was no longer my grandmother. She was just an ordinary old woman who was no longer in her right mind. She raised her left arm, with which she held an imaginary violin, and pretended to stroke its strings with an imaginary bow that she gripped with her right hand. I will never get over that image of her.

"Your grandmother aroused the vanity of a beautiful woman in you. She was beautiful, but you are not. You are an ugly woman with the vanity of a beautiful woman. You don't understand that, and that's the trouble with you," my husband used to tell me.

When I was growing up, I gradually yielded to the will of my grandmother. My mother could not understand how a child as disobedient as I was could have become so compliant in my grandmother's presence. As I had told Ileana, I would try to please my grandmother at all costs. I paid attention to everything that she did. I watched how she ate, how she would wipe her hands on a towel, how she folded her clean laundry, how she shelled beans or tied up bundles of camomile for the winter. When she took her weekly bath, she would lock the door and seal the windows, even if it was dark out. I was always surprised that she had such slim ankles; how could they support the weight of her ample hips? I really loved the winter evenings when she would take a knife and scrape the calluses off her feet, which was something my mother never did.

I had trouble believing Aunt Cecilia when she speculated that my grandfather had a mistress. But it could have been true. He was a massive man, but as docile as a puppy, blessed with immense patience. He was never in a hurry, he got along with everyone, he didn't shout or ever get angry. His greatest passion in life had been the horses. Apart from that, he was very ordinary, except that he was my grandpa.

The way our love focuses in on someone, for no apparent reason, is very bizarre. It is mysterious and spontaneous. And so is the way we begin to love someone who doesn't deserve it or to whom we mean nothing. How can you respect someone who doesn't give a damn about your existence or your feelings? The way you feel, Ileana. I know that you don't give a damn, that you never really listen to what I'm saying.

"I've remained a stranger to you," Mihai would say. "It's as if I were living with someone I didn't know. Tell me, at least from time to time, that you love me! Is it such torture for you to say nice things to me?"

Under cover of darkness, my ancestors Petre and Marie had waged an endless war: it was a biblical war, an epic war signalling the beginning of the world.

I think that I entered the history of my great-grandparents only after the sun went down. I had heard most of the particulars from Aunt Cecilia, who liked to concentrate on the shameful parts. She was the one who had told me about the torture that Marie had endured because of her beauty, her widowhood, her loneliness, and her refusal to get remarried. My grandmother Stana, named after Marie's big sister, held nothing against Petre for hitting Marie: my grandmother had always been constrained by what ought to be done. I entered this history at night because, in the light of day, my vision was blurred by tears and regret for poor Marie. I was ashamed of her bruises, the beatings she took. During the day, it was too painful to read all the letters of the human alphabet. The story would become diluted and Petre's love for Marie would lose its mythical and obscure meaning.

In my dreams, Marie became a woman of dazzling beauty and that man, who came from another village to kiss her feet, embodied the power and virility of biblical patriarchs.

I didn't ever want to wake up again. I was becoming Marie, beautiful Marie, my grandmother's mother, who would ramble barefoot on the dusty roads, or across the freshly mown fields driving a small herd of goats. I liked the torture she endured, which became my own torture. I had chosen violence, which threatened her life every step of the way. It was a life that unfolded outdoors, under the heat and light of the sun, in a world that had not yet lost its meaning and its reason for being.

My love story with Petre had begun in a shack on the edge of the lake. I was living in the house I had inherited from my first husband, with three narrow rooms, surrounded by a yard full of greenery, a small vegetable garden and three rows of onions, a space enclosed by a tall wooden fence for the cart, which had been abandoned after the pair of oxen were sold. I only had a sickly donkey who wasn't able to move the massive cart with wooden wheels.

The story began almost as soon as I became a widow. My first husband had died from tuberculosis the previous year. He died a slow death, tormenting and torturing his children, cursing me the minute I slipped away from his deathbed. He was sorry he couldn't carry me off with him, to hell. But now, someone else threatened to disturb my harmonious and peaceful existence, the female silence around me. A man once again burst noisily into my beautiful and solitary life. He came knocking at my door every night trying to force me to take him. I had said no once and for all, but he would not take no for an answer. He continued his nightly surveillance while I watched out for him, camouflaged behind the window. I watched through a thick curtain while the master and his horse waited for me in the darkness on the other side of the fence. Hidden in the house, my hands crossed over my belly, I kept watch for hours and hours on end, fending off this undesirable man, who had come to bring me trouble and unhappiness. Why should I be ashamed of being a widow with two children? I just wanted to live alone in my house, alone with desires that no one had yet satisfied. A woman's desires can only be satisfied in her dreams: this is what no man, neither young nor old, could comprehend.

During my hours of keeping watch, I would sit with my elbows on the table, on which there was a plate with a piece of bread that my children had saved for the next day. The strong-smelling kerosene lamp had been blown out. I scratched at the mosquito bites on my hands and feet.

I was waiting for sleep to come, but I was not yet drowsy. I was waiting for the man to leave, but he refused to budge one step before dawn. I would try to swallow the lump in my throat, but it wouldn't go away. Like every other night, I could not fall asleep until I saw him leave, just as I began to hear the villagers shouting in the street as they headed out for the fields, with their wives and children still fast asleep in the back of their carts.

According to Aunt Cecilia, the match had been arranged by Stana, Marie's older sister. I had kept her in my story, too, so that I could badger her every day. Is that why she couldn't sleep either? Had she lost her appetite because she was worried about finding happiness for me? Because I didn't want to be forced to marry this man? No, it's true, I didn't want to marry him, and I didn't want to be made to marry just anyone. Most of all, I didn't want to leave my fortune to you, Stana, so that you could inherit everything I had amassed all my life.

I felt certain that I was contemplating the same sky as my great-grandmother, the sky in which the full moon had risen. By this time of year, the Big Dipper had changed its handle while the Little Dipper had lost one of the points of its bowl. The Gemini twins were embracing one another while Sagittarius was pulling back his bow. I was looking at the windowpane with the same panic as Marie, who would shudder at the slightest unexpected noise. She thought she had heard a horse snorting. Petre, who was still planted behind the door, had taken off his hat and grabbed the horse by the bridle. Like Marie, I saw him gently stroking the horse above its nostrils. Suddenly he turned his head toward the darkened windows. He knew full well at which window I was standing guard. He knew I would not leave the house today or tomorrow. Despite his persistence, I had no feelings for him. Even worse, I believed he was a liar.

He had made my head spin with all his talk about his riches. Everything was better at his place than at ours: the houses, horses, carts, potatoes, milk, bread, and children. He had told me several times that he had two dairy cows. And, above all, he wanted me to know that he didn't want any of my possessions, that was not why he wanted to marry me. If I liked, I could leave my fortune to my sister. A real gentleman, he asked me to follow him right away, while still in my nightgown.

But I warned him that he could not come into my house. Under no circumstances could he cross the threshold. I told him he was forbidden to breach my sanctuary. Inside, I would be vulnerable, subject to his whims and those of others. My little house was all I had to protect me and ensure that I remained free.

It was not just my sister Stana who was involved in our lives. The entire village knew my slightest movements by heart, predicted my desires, bet on the outcome of the story, plotted against me, and took the stranger's side. Everyone asked Stana questions, and she was just as surprised as I was by the antipathy directed against me. She didn't think I should reject the man, but she didn't see how it was the business of other people. Why would the villagers know better than me?

What bothered the village people most was the failure of Marie's first marriage to Petre. Urged to do so by Stana, Marie had agreed to follow Petre to his village. But by the next day, she had returned to her house on the edge of the lake. Now, all the women were asking my sister,

"Why did your sister go back home? I thought that she had married that man, who came to get her on horseback, and who spent the whole night at her door."

"Yes, it's true that she went with him, but now she's back," my embarrassed sister answered.

"But why? Perhaps he beat her. Was he right to hit her? What do you think?"

"But why would he have beaten her? And, mainly, when? I don't think that they even had time to talk to one another. Don't you see that they were only together for one night? You know how she is, she doesn't say much. She is so stubborn. She really deserved to get slapped around."

"I heard that he keeps coming back for her. Especially at night. Is that true?"

"Yes, it's true. He still comes. He comes and he stays at her gate until dawn."

"And what does she do? Doesn't she ever go out to speak to him?"

"Never, my dear. As soon as it gets dark, she goes into the house with her children, closes the door, and doesn't go out again until morning."

"And what does he do?"

"He stays outside, he stands there and waits. His horse grazes on the grass at the edge of the ditch while he stands there, with his hat pulled down over his nose, staring at the windows."

"But why don't you talk to her? Don't you ask her what's going on?"

"Oh my God, how many times have I spoken to her? How many times have we argued about it? From the beginning I've said to her, as her older sister, 'Marie, what are you doing? What are you thinking? You are going back and forth, from one village to another, with your dowry. Why don't you like that man, he's the best match for you, don't you see? He has everything he needs, he could give you anything you want. He has two cows, imagine, who else do you know with two cows?' And do you know what she replied, that foolish girl? 'Cows, get out of here!' Yes, that's what she said, she told me that, to me, the person who raised her from childhood, after our mother died. 'He doesn't even own the hide of two cows, that's the kind of man you want me to marry. I have a little house and these two hands, but I would never, never tell a lie about what I own. No one should brag about something they don't have.' Yes, perhaps, he just says that he has cows. What do I know? She should be happy that she doesn't have to work in the sun all day mowing the grass to feed the cattle. Do you know how much a cow eats? But no, she is fixated on his lies. He may not have cows, but he has a big house, two beautiful horses, grapevines in his yard, and another vineyard in the fields. If he told her that he owned a castle, should she believe him?"

Since that incident, Marie had always lived in fear. Her life would never be the same again. She would never again be at peace. She lived with the memory of the nights when the stranger stood guard at her doorway relentlessly. She could picture the horse snoring behind its master, who wore his cap pulled down over his forehead. She could see herself watching, frightened, through the curtains. She quaked at every sound, even in daytime. Every time she heard footsteps, or horses trotting behind her, she would gasp with fear. The voices of men she didn't know sent cold shivers down her spine. In the fields, at the well, around the grocery store, she was followed and watched all the time.

As for me, I was just as miserable as poor Marie, who had lost her widow's serenity. Because I couldn't go out, I lived my life within the walls of my house, just as cloistered as she had been. I couldn't leave the house on Sunday or holidays, or take part in the ladies' chitchat. I couldn't even sit out on my stoop on the little wooden bench my husband had carved.

Petre followed me around like a dog even though he knew full well that I didn't know anyone, that I wouldn't flirt with any other man. But he wanted me to feel him, to know every second of my life that he existed, that he would always exist, and that no one else would kiss me or possess me. I lived in the same fear as Marie that one day this man would lie in wait for me somewhere in a secluded spot. He would choose a moment when everyone had left the fields, when there was no one left to hear me if I cried out, yelled, or struggled.

Stana must have seen how furious this man actually was and how dangerous he could be for the peace of a household. She couldn't have been stupid enough not to know. Petre was like a bull that had broken its chain. He could go to hell with his two cows!

It was Aunt Cecilia who had so vividly recounted the first trip that Marie had made to Petre's house and what had happened there. Was Aunt Cecilia right? Well, yes! For sure. She always told the truth about the private lives of others, about what happened behind closed doors. She was telling the truth about how sad Marie had been when she was loading her things onto the cart parked in front of her house.

Petre was taking everything that the woman was telling him to take and carrying it all outside. But he flatly refused to take the beds. He looked at the one in which Marie's first husband had lain suffering for two and a half years. How could he desire the body of a woman and be afraid of the sin that was inscribed in a few pieces of wood? Marie began to dismantle the beds by herself when Petre refused to do it. Once again, he told her in a loud, gruff voice that they were not going to take a single board from her house. Aunt Cecilia relayed the thoughts that Marie might have had about this man, 'Damn you,' she would tell him, 'You want to give them to my sister, the person who pushed you into my life. She is impatiently waiting for me to leave so that she can lay her hands on my goat and my little donkey. And now you expect me to leave her the planks of wood my bed is made of. May she burn even before she gets to hell!'

And I continued to relive this forgotten story on my own.

I pictured myself seated next to Petre on a plain board placed between the two sides of the cart. The three children were squabbling behind us, among the trunks in which I had thrown my dowry together. But the two of us remained silent all along the way. He, in particular, had not uttered a word. I snuck a glance at his dirty shirt, which was worn out in the back, at his greasy hair, which was full of dandruff, and at his pants, which shone with grease at the knees where he placed his hands. He kept his hat pulled down over his face, so you couldn't see his eyes.

After travelling for a few hours, we arrived at his house. Around it was an orchard of poorly tended plum trees and an abundance of quack grass. In the yard, a little stream of water flowed out from under a pile of garbage. We unloaded my belongings and carried them into the guest room, which had been kept clean. The children went out into the street and played with the neighbouring kids.

I was tired and sat down on the edge of the bed, my arms dangling. He went to water the horses. Then he came back into the house. Pinned to the doorway, he observed me as I sat alone and sad, ready to get up and leave the place. My headscarf had slipped down, revealing my pinned-up hair. He told me to cover my hair back up.

I asked him how to heat water so that we could get washed. He replied that it was Thursday and that we would have to wait two more days until Saturday.

I prepared dinner, but it was very difficult. I had to ask him for everything—salt, matches, flour, pots, plates—because I didn't know where to find anything. We were in a bad mood, embarrassed, and didn't look at one another or say a word as we ate. His son, who had not washed his hands before sitting down at the table, looked at me wide-eyed. He had burned himself on the polenta and his father had given him a slap. I wasn't allowed to wash the boy before bedtime. I said nothing, but I washed my own children with cold water, from top to bottom.

The children lay down in a single bed, on the other side of the table, huddled up together, and fell asleep. After that, we made love for a few minutes, after which he turned his back on me.

In the morning, he left for the fields with his horses while I secretly admitted to a neighbour that I wanted to go back to my village and that I needed help to be able to do that.

When I got back home, I had a vicious fight with my sister Stana. I had taken the goat and donkey back from her, and I ordered her to leave me alone. Stana persevered. She now came to my house to help me with all the chores. I was tired of trying to get rid of her, of chasing her away all the time, and I ended up letting her stay around.

What a mistake it had been to follow that man! How could I have accepted that burden? I had been wrong not to go with him from the beginning. But even worse, I was wrong to have left him afterward. That man would never leave me alone. He would never leave me in peace, not for the rest of my life. He would never marry another woman. He would pursue me with his horse, with his hat pulled down over his forehead, for the rest of my days. And if I married him, there would be no woman worse off than me.

After a few days, I made up with Stana. Shedding tears, I told her about my misadventures in the stranger's house.

"He wore such a dirty shirt, and his son was covered in dust. I asked him where he kept the bathtub, where he kept the tripod and kettle for heating bath water. 'We like to get washed.' That's how I put it, I swear. He looked at me with contempt. He was surprised that I would think about having a bath on a Thursday. Can you imagine? On Sunday, he would put on a clean shirt and not change it till the following Saturday."

The first time I met Petre, after we had separated, was one week later. I plucked up my courage and left the house to do some shopping in the centre of the village. I was returning from the grocery store at sundown, carrying two parcels. This time, I did not take the busy main street in the village, but a sideroad that ran along the river.

If something was going to happen, let it happen as soon as possible. I lingered on the narrow path, in the shade of the willows. Finally, I wanted to tell that man the truth. Tell him once and for all that I didn't want him.

"You are no better or worse than the others—I would begin—but I don't want you. I don't want anyone else either. I no longer want to tire myself out by looking after your house or any home other than mine. I don't want to be beaten and humiliated, scorned, and insulted. I don't want to see my children running away from you, quivering with fear in your presence. I am well aware of what awaits me, after the nights you have spent standing at my door. It's not that I don't like you, I don't know whether I like you or not anymore, but I just don't want you. And I don't want to have any more children." I had been composing this speech in my head for a long time and was preparing to say the words out loud.

All of a sudden, I heard the clippety-clop of horseshoes on the little trail behind me. It was him! I waited for him to come close, I even went to stand on the side of the road. He got off his horse, took me in his arms, and lifted me up onto the saddle. Then he mounted the horse behind me. I rode side-saddle, leaning my shoulder against his chest, my hip pressed up against his stomach. The most intimate, the most indecent pose possible. I held my packages tight against my breast. His shirt was just as dirty as the week before. He had not changed it. Before going into the little street that runs in front of my house, I tried to dismount so I wouldn't be seen so close to him. At that very moment, he grabbed my shoulder and kept me pinned to him. With one hand holding on to the reins, he grabbed my breasts with his other hand and squeezed his long, booted legs around my hips.

I don't know who might have noticed me in his company, but the next day a few of the women once again pestered my sister with questions about it. One of them had told her,

"I heard that the dirty rascal took your sister to his house, that he carried her off on horseback along the path that runs through the willows."

"I don't know anything, my dear," replied my sister Stana. "Those are just rumours, and, as you well know, people do make things up."

Stana was just as disappointed as I was. I told her how the man had made love to me the night I spent at his house.

"Once the children were asleep, he took off his shirt. But he didn't tell me to get undressed. He just pulled my skirt up over my thighs. He was the one who pulled my knees apart. I didn't want him, and he no longer desired me. Yet, he put himself between my thighs. He was dirty and he knew I was thinking only about that. Instead of penetrating me, he could have slapped my soft face. He was certainly asking himself why I was so beautiful. Why my body was so seductive, why my armpits didn't stink, why my skin was so fair and my shirt so clean. I turned my head to one side, so I wouldn't have to look at him. If my eyes had met his, even once, he would have melted. The contempt I felt would have wounded him to the very core. He turned his back to me, pretending to be satisfied and indifferent. But I knew that he wanted me again, but in a different way, a more tender way. He was waiting for my fingers to stroke his shoulder. He hoped that I would call him by his name and that I would get him to turn toward me. Instead, I got out of bed and looked around for an old towel to wipe away the thick liquid that was flowing between my thighs."

Stana, who had been a widow for more than ten years, didn't understand any of that, and couldn't see why I was offended. Could a woman hope for more than a few seconds of attention from a man? She apologized, although she still didn't see why she was wrong.

"Marie, he's not that bad. You don't know him, you don't know how he was at the beginning when he came to my house to ask for your hand in marriage. He was so nice, with his hat pulled over his neck. He was a bit dirty, he hadn't shaved for a few days, and he was tired and perhaps starving. He sat on the edge of the bed, shyly. He took his hat off and twirled it around in his hands. He talked to me about you, he said he had heard that you had been a widow for a year, that he had seen you and had fallen in love with you, that you were a very reasonable and beautiful woman who didn't chase after men. He wanted to marry you. He tried to act properly. First of all, he talked to your family, so that you would not be shamed, so that people would not talk about you behind your back. He knew that you would have trouble getting used to the neighbours and a new village. But he said that he would let you do whatever you wanted: visit us whenever you liked, keep your house, leave your farm to your children. He only wanted you to be kind to him, good to his son, who had lost his mother. If you had seen how shy and polite he was, you would understand why I agreed with him, why I was happy to have found such a pleasant husband for you."

Yes, perhaps I should have believed that my sister was concerned for my well-being. I should have known because she was crying as she spoke to me.

"You didn't even want to listen to me or hear anything about a new marriage. You stuck to your guns, insisting that you had your home and children, that you had already had one husband and had no desire for another. He would come to my house every night and I could see how his attitude was changing. He no longer removed his hat, he didn't want to sit down, he became less and less soft-spoken, he would just stand in the doorway and try to bully me. He told me, too, about the cows, about his house and his beautiful cart. But what could I do? I believed that it was in your interest to go with him, to start a new family. Do you think that I didn't want to remarry? I would have gone off with anybody, even a Roma, if someone had asked me to. Do you think getting old alone is such a great accomplishment?"

They kept arguing about it until Marie decided to leave her house one night to go talk to Petre. Aunt Cecilia was once again a marvellous storyteller as she continued with this part of the saga, revelling in every detail.

Marie had put her skirt on over her nightshirt. After covering her hair with a black headscarf, she went out. With his hat pulled down over his forehead, he had not budged from the doorway. She said to him, "Petre, I don't want to marry you."

"But who asked you to marry me?"

"Well then, why are you coming to my door?"

"Because I love your door."

"Do you want me to become the laughingstock of the village? Do you want everyone to make fun of me?"

"Laugh about what? And do you care about everyone else? You come and go as you like. But you know, you came to my house, you slept in my bed, you cooked for me. From now on, I have a right to you. You are my wife, a woman who has left her own home."

Marie had to accept the words of her sister, who had also understood her error.

"A woman can't do what you have done, Marie," my sister said to me. "If you don't love a man, how can you tell him that he is not clean? It isn't possible to give someone a piece of your mind if you don't have feelings for him, my little sister."

Before dawn, I was dreaming about the last episode of this story. The ladies of the village were saying to my sister,

"I heard that the fool took your sister and beat her to death."

"That's a lie, my dear, you shouldn't believe everything you hear."

"But what a lie! I saw her with a black eye and her arm in a sling."

"She bumped into the corner of a cupboard. I was at her place when it happened."

I had relived, with as much pain as Marie, the thrashing he had given her the first time on the edge of the wheat field, where he had snuck up on her. I was suffering and crying as much as she had a hundred years earlier. Petre was beating me and laughing all the while, as if I were his plaything. He looked as if he intended to stroke me but instead punched me with his heavy fists. Then he took my head in his hands, brought his face close to mine, and breathed in my breath. In fact, he wanted to kiss my bloody lips. This was the only time he allowed himself to become tender and affectionate, moved by my black-and-blue cheeks and tear-filled eyes. Having only ever experienced rejection from me, this was his only chance to get close to me, to be intimate with me and my body.

I stayed like that, an inert mass in the middle of the path. Before closing my eyes as I lay on the ground, I could make out an anthill very close to my forehead.

More than anything, I loved the story of my great-grandmother, as my grandmother had begun to tell it and as Aunt Cecilia had finished it. I loved it because it was a story in which a man's love becomes deadly, in which the woman puts up no resistance, in which she can only suffer flagellation and persecution, even though they are motivated by love. In all these stories, the odour of sperm merged with the odour of animals and sour male sweat. There was nothing but pain and copulation. Men and women, with no room for beauty, tenderness, or friendship between them.

I woke up again with a start. A young man was leaning over me, his face almost glued to mine. He was staring at me. He had found me and was now trying to get me up on my feet, against my will.

What was he looking for in my house, in broad daylight? I had told him not to cross the threshold of my home. I had told him so many times that I didn't want to marry him, not him or anyone else.

But no, it was Mihai. He had taken Daniel to Bucharest. After several days without rain, the roads were drier and, today, he was able to bring me food, warm clothing, and an electric heater.

We couldn't talk to each other anymore. Both of us were struggling desperately to find the right words to say, but it was impossible. He stayed with me for a few hours, but he was anxious to leave the village again before sundown. The only thing I really grasped was that Daniel was now staying in Buzau with my cousin.

November

In November, George helped me to get an abortion.

He had come to see me because Dinut had told him about me, hinting that I was a bit cuckoo. According to him, I was wandering through the village, all alone, barefoot and dressed too lightly for the terrible cold. I was astonished that people could take such delight in bad-mouthing me given how reserved they seemed. Since arriving here, I had not been able to exchange two words with anyone. And yet, all the villagers were aware of my presence. But where did they get the idea that I was crazy? That's how George found out about me. Was he coming just to check out the rumours? Especially since I had seemed of sound mind to him when we had met in the Rosiori train station.

When he burst into my bedroom, I was beginning to come back to my senses, after the amnesia I had experienced in October. I was eating better, and from time to time I even washed my hands and face. My clothes were still filthy, but it was warm inside the house, which made everything more bearable. I stayed in bed all day, looking out the window. Outside, the scenery had changed completely. That's how it would stay until spring. The trees were totally bare, the briar was gone, ravaged by the morning mist, and the ground was covered in wet leaves. There was not a trace of greenery. In the afternoon, when the fog lifted, I could see dilapidated fences and crumbling walls in the distance. It was much more depressing than in summer. I was petrified by the silence around me. I was even afraid to make the slightest noise myself.

George had entered the house without warning. He had found me huddled up against the wall, with a thick blanket pulled up to my chin, spending most of the day staring out the window. I had set the radiator up in the middle of the room. On the table lay the packages of food that Mihai had brought. He had returned two weeks after his first visit, but without Daniel. I hadn't asked him to bring the boy along, either. I didn't miss him. I was no longer able to take care of anyone. I hadn't asked Mihai whether Daniel was still in Buzau with my cousin, or whether Mihai was looking after him. It was his problem. And Mihai didn't ask me to come back to the city either.

Oh, how I appreciated his lack of affection! It would have been much more painful had he been emotional and excessively attentive. I no longer wanted anyone to worry about me. Above all, I didn't want to hear anything about the future, about marriage, about the city, about love. The only thing I wished for was this immense space empty of desire. Mihai was letting me live serenely, like a ghost. It was so pleasant to have no one to call me to account, no one to question me about anything.

I was deeply disturbed by George's arrival. Not that I didn't want to see him. On the contrary, I was really happy. I was so pleased by his appearance that I imagined it had been arranged by God himself. Why hadn't I taken advantage of his regular presence here? I had completely forgotten that George was the other face of my past. George and Ilie had been polar opposites, the north and south of my life. Although they had been buried for a long time under the ice floes of my past, they were now emerging so easily.

George's presence forced me to learn how to speak again. I had not uttered a complete sentence since September. My tongue had lain swollen between my teeth like a decaying mollusk and my vocal cords had become coated with a thick mucus that was like corrosive rust. When asked a question, I would reply with a broad smile. My entire face offered proof that I was happy that he had finally found me. How I had missed him without realizing it.

Our meeting on the railway platform had been so ambiguous for both of us. I couldn't remember what he had said to me, not even if he was married or if he was working. He told me, over again, that he was a dental technician, married, and childless. I was willing to hear him say anything. I was not yet ready to talk about myself, and he wasn't either, not this time. He didn't ask for specifics. I appreciated his discretion immensely.

But out of the blue, I asked him to help me get an abortion, to take me to a doctor in the city, even to the local quack, as long as he could get rid of the baby. Perhaps he could take me to the hospital where he worked in Craiova. I had to tear this embryo out of my body as soon as possible. I had neither the desire nor the power to continue this pregnancy, although for two months I had been convinced that I would give birth to this child and that my happiness depended on it. As soon as I saw George appear on my doorstep, I realized that this was just a huge mistake and that he had come explicitly for my redemption and my deliverance.

He agreed to help and said nothing about my pregnancy or my decision. The next day, we left for Craiova. We went directly from the train station to the hospital, where I patiently waited my turn in the waiting room, alongside several gloomy and anxious patients. I was at peace as I went in for the procedure. Under anesthesia, I had almost the same visions as I had had in October. My head hurt terribly and I could feel the assistant's hand on my mouth. Right after the operation, as I was beginning to wake up, I saw George near me, but he didn't dare touch me. I was moved to a recovery room, separated from the large ward where other women lay on their stomachs moaning. By three o'clock in the afternoon, I was much improved. George took care of the discharge formalities, and then we walked to his apartment, which was in the neighbourhood, stopping to rest on every available bench.

His wife came home from work very late. She was not very surprised to see me lying on the living room couch, less surprised than I might have been in the same situation. She made supper and we all ate together. George talked at length about how dental prostheses are manufactured.

The next day, I refused to stay any longer. George took me to the station and stayed with me until the train arrived. Before we parted, he made me promise for the umpteenth time to remember to take painkillers. He had put a sweater and some blouses belonging to his wife into a small bag, along with two chocolate bars. Everyone was spoiling me, seducing me with treats, as if I were a child. They quickly spotted my weakness for sweets from the way in which I looked at them, fixated by them, when I saw them on grocery shelves, in pastry shop windows, or in the hands of young kids.

I got better soon, without any lasting effects. To avoid blood clots, I took a little walk every day along the garden path. I also dutifully took antibiotics and slept all the time. I slept deeply, peacefully, without any nightmares. Every night, I was happy to go back into the story of my great-grandmother, Marie, to construct segments without violence. I lived only for those dreams, postponing their resolution as much as possible.

Marie avoided running into Petre, but he followed her from afar. He would beat her viciously and then give her the time she needed for her wounds and bruises to heal. I tolerated the tension in their relationship, but as soon as things took a violent turn and looked as if they could have a tragic ending, I started all over from the beginning. First, I went back over their move, their first trip in the cart with the three children behind them, their first night of lovemaking, and their hostile glances at one another. When Marie went back to her village, the man's diabolical pursuit began. Her sister Stana came around to believing Marie's side of the story and finally understood the man's rage and blind passion. She tried to be a buffer between their story and the rest of the world, people who wouldn't stop spying on them, lurking in corners. She did her best to assuage the unfortunate lover's furor and impetuousness, but nothing could be done to make him more attractive to her little sister, who was impervious to the charm of all men. Since Stana was always around, she was the only one who could protect Marie from the increasingly intense oppression of the stranger.

How I loved living in the little house by the lake, with my children, in blessed solitude! And how I loved the world in which women were supposed to be subservient, and in which they tried to rebel, but without success. I loved the rage and fury of my great-grandmother but also her conviction that her defeat was in fact normal. Yes, Marie knew full well how it would all end, because no other outcome was possible. But she wanted to take advantage of her freedom to try to avoid her fate. Even if it was all for naught.

And suddenly, that man had an insane desire for this woman, for this one particular woman. He then circled in closer to her until she could smell his hunter's breath and hear the panting of a man on the verge of intercourse.

Oh, my God, how cruel I was to give him, and him alone, the right to love. I had numbed Marie's senses, crazy desires, and irrational thoughts. No, certainly not, Marie would never want him. He alone would have prostrated himself, crawled to her feet just to get her to cast a sympathetic look at him, to make a brief welcoming gesture. But the woman loved only her solitude and freedom to sleep alone, in her own bed.

Marie was alarmed by Petre's burning breath. She looked around, searching for a place to hide. In some of the stories, I even went so far as to imagine rape. Yes, I liked to see Marie possessed against her will, against her wishes. Crucified on the naked earth, in the attic, or on the riverbank, penetrated by force. She didn't resist in any way, knowing it would be useless to do so. Petre was good at choosing the moments when the human race seemed to have disappeared from the face of the earth, when there was nothing left but an immense appetite for copulation, for physical possession.

Nonetheless, I couldn't rely on this plot too many times. Every time it looked like things were headed in this direction, I invented new misadventures. I had them meet in the village, at the mill, or at the weekly fair held in Radomiresti. He sometimes forced her to ride on the merry-go-round. Similarly, he made her eat sausages and a slice of melon with him. When she refused, he offered to buy her a skirt and treats for the children. But Marie would accept nothing from him, except under duress.

Why did Marie like to be so contrary? Why did she only respond to his desires when raped, forced, brutalized. Why had she chosen to wage such a war?

I sometimes tried another variation. After being taken to Petre's village with her children and dowry, Marie never left her new husband's house again. She had resigned herself to staying there, to spending her life with Petre and his son, who lived in fear of his father. I imagined the existence of a couple in which the husband was not only unloved, but also had to endure the contempt of a beautiful woman who regarded him as an unclean, vicious, and violent brute. But things did not go that well. Simply put, I didn't like that version of the story. I was satisfied with the quest, fuelled by hate and anger: Petre's dogged effort to track this woman across sun-drenched stretches of prairie, along dusty trails, through cornfields, apple orchards, and vineyards where the grapes exuded their spicy odour. I wanted Marie to be the game and Petre the hunter. And what I loved most was her heroic resistance to the siege. Her big sister Stana was convinced that it would be a thousand times preferable if Marie went with him immediately, because in any case she would do so eventually. What was the point of all this? Marie, beautiful Marie, my ravishing, magical, and beloved great-grandmother, defended herself tenaciously.

During my days of convalescence, I had let the story get bogged down. I was waiting until I felt better to set out in battle once again.

George came the following week and brought me a pile of newspapers. However, I had no desire to read the news. I wasn't at all interested in what had happened over the previous months. Only then did George become curious enough to ask me whether I had really been living like this since the summer, doing nothing, absolutely nothing.

"Yes," I answered. "I've been doing nothing."

What else could he say? How could he convince me that this situation was terrible, especially since I wanted to keep on living like this? Didn't I want him to tell me what had happened during my weeks of apathy, during my absence from the world? No, I was not at all interested. I was like my parents who had lived here without knowing anything about what was happening beyond the fields of wheat and corn. And what better proof than their lives. Yes, it was possible to live this way, without knowing anything, without affecting the course of the world in any way, without experiencing any concern for it. How could you be surprised that anything was possible?

"At least you should know that we have a new president," he continued insistently.

Even that didn't interest me. And yet, I found the piece of news amusing. I was the only person in the entire country who didn't know there was a new president.

George was adamant about bringing me a radio. What good would it do? I had never been much of a radio fan. For that, I would have had to be educated, trained to understand the information I was hearing, but I wasn't. The only thing that made my life bearable was the story of my great-grandmother.

Unlike me, George came from a family of intellectuals, or so they were regarded in our village. His mother and even grandfather had been nurses. Despite their profession, they had not earned the respect of the villagers since George, like his mother, was the child of an adulterous relationship. Besides, patients were terrified of getting needles from his mother. She had a heavy hand, they said. During the time when we were classmates, his mother had had three lovers. People said that the last one had left the village with burned hands because she had pushed him against a hot stove. George, as opposed to his mother, was as gentle as a lamb. When we were in school together, I had liked him a lot. There was a constant and lasting friendship between us. We were never jealous of each other, as adolescents often were. We may have had more lively disagreements from time to time, which was actually one way of proving our love for each other. But during the time we were friends, we hardly ever touched each other. In class, I sometimes caught him staring at me.

He was a rather ugly boy, with a big mouth, puffy lips, flat temples, and a head that protruded at the back. I liked him a lot the way he was, nonetheless, with his hair cropped short and slicked back, with the docile temperament of a girl, and with tight clothes. He didn't arouse any vulgar or obscene thoughts in me. All my erotic fantasies were triggered by Ilie, whom I always believed I would marry one day.

George sat in the front row of the class. I was very happy and calm knowing he was there, where I could see him. Our friendship was threatened on only one occasion, when I rubbed his face with sandpaper. His scratches had become infected, and his mother had come to the school to speak to the principal. But when I was called up in front of the class, George burst into tears. I immediately forgave him for talking about it at home. From that time on, even his mother began to think I was nice. Whenever I greeted her, she responded in a special way, with the kind of strange solidarity that develops between mothers and the girls their sons are hanging out with.

George and I now resumed our friendship the way we had left it, when we parted because we were each going off to the lycée. But how he had aged! We had always been so open with one another that I wasn't afraid to ask him why he had grown old so quickly. His face looked particularly wrinkled, with mouth and eyes that were encircled with deep lines and sparse hair that had turned almost completely white. He looked like he was in his forties whereas he was just two years older than I was. He had been sick while he was still in primary school and had fallen a bit behind as a result.

He wasn't angry at such a question. He responded gently. That was the way it was: the men in his family looked older than other people. But what men was he talking about? His grandfather was a red head, whose right foot had been amputated, it's true, but who was otherwise in good health. Who knows? Perhaps he was talking about his father, whom he had not known, to my knowledge.

George kept his promise. The following week, he brought me a small radio and showed me how to select the stations I wanted. I listened to him carefully, but once he had left, I left the radio tuned to the one station he had picked. I wasn't lucid enough to decode what I was hearing on the radio. Words tickled my ears and put me to sleep like the hum of buzzing bees.

When he came to see me, George would make the coffee himself. He had brought me a little coffee pot and an immersion heater. How happy I was to see that George had the same little vice as me. We drank our coffee with religious fervour. First of all, we would sniff the pleasant coffee aroma. Then, we would lift the cup to our lips and drink the black liquid as if we were taking Holy Communion.

His visits grew more and more frequent and brought me back to life. The innocent drug brought me short moments of euphoria, in the company of this ugly and almost old man. He would leave me enough coffee for a week, but I wasn't even capable of preparing it. I would drink leftover coffee after he left, and then I would begin to talk to myself. That is how I recovered my ability to speak. When we got together, I would become more and more chatty and coherent. George had no inkling that he was the cause of the change. Each time he came, he found me a little livelier.

During one of those visits, I suggested to George that we have sex. Yes, we should f**k. No, we should make love.

"Why?" he asked, as if I was insisting that he have dinner with me when he wasn't hungry.

Unfortunately, I wasn't hungry either. But why not?

I imagined how hard he must be taking such an indecent proposition, formulated so directly by a woman. But, actually, why did I always have to think about the reaction of other people? Why didn't I just tell him that I wanted to get laid?

He agreed. The way he always agreed to make the coffee meticulously. Yes! We got undressed, but not completely, and we slipped under the covers. I didn't even have the decency to be quiet about how dirty I was. George, in turn, admitted that he had sweaty armpits.

We didn't manage to make love. Instead of kissing and fondling each other, we talked about our bodies and their defects.

The following week, everything happened almost normally, with discretion and decency. George's body had its own special beauty, the hidden beauty of a person with an ugly face. He was thin, but not at all unattractive. His skin exuded a sweet-and-sour scent, as if he ate sandalwood. If I touched him, I would seek out the plump and tender parts. His body seemed to have been emptied of its bones and felt as light as a balloon. He caressed me tenderly and would stop at the slightest hesitation on my part. He would worry, every time, and ask,

"Does that hurt?"

He was always afraid to cause me pain. We would only make love if I were willing, and we would stop as soon as I showed the least sign of fatigue or discomfort. When he looked at me, I could tell that he was urging me to enjoy the sex, and to come.

We had gone to bed because it was impossible not to. We had given in to the old stereotype of a man and a woman left alone in a room together having no choice but to end up copulating. Whatever happened, things always finished that way. When they didn't, the relationship would remain sterile and empty. It was as if we had abdicated our primal and most important role in life until now. For unsophisticated people, the drive to reproduce remained more vital than the urge to protect oneself.

Despite some individual progress, no one, finally, could escape this temptation. It was cold out, we had very little to eat and, what's more, we had nothing else to do. We were all doomed to live in our cold and dark dwellings and reproduce.

But why had I become so fertile?

December

The following month I realized that I was once again pregnant.

The slightest contact with a man made me germinate, leaving me with an embryo. I had become a kind of Universal Mother, who could be fertilized by the mere breath of a male. I believed that it was Petre, my great-grandfather, Marie's nocturnal hunter, who had impregnated me, rather than the sperm of the man next door.

It was impossible that this George, who was so weak and timid and with whom I had copulated so gently, with thousands of precautions taken between the sheets, would be capable of such an act. I wanted to be loved by biblical patriarchs like long-haired Samson. How was it possible to procreate without any suffering, any battles, any opposition? What would become of the child I gave birth to if I didn't make the fury and rage of conception flow in its veins? If I had not been taken violently from behind, if the man had not bitten my neck just as he was pumping his semen into my vagina? Why had my uterus sucked up his viscous fluid like a pump, and why were his juices already turning sour and diluted? Where on my body had the bites, signs of the beginning of the greedy act, left their mark after intercourse?

Nothing, there was nothing of the kind! Instead, I saw embarrassed looks, pained expressions, shy eyes begging for forgiveness for everything that had taken place, but should not have happened. After a dirty act of copulation, we were only concerned with precarious hygiene. Most of the time, the bedroom was so cold that we remained immobile under the covers, where we became boiling hot between the unclean bedsheets.

In mid-December, the first snow fell, followed by a terrible deep freeze that covered my windows from top to bottom with a thin layer of frost. The radiator was running day and night, except for short periods when I turned it off so it could cool down.

George had introduced a bit of order into my life. He had moved the table from the middle of the room and placed it against the wall. Supplies were now in another room, the old kitchen. He had brought plastic plates, which I used only when he was there. I was also happy he had brought thick woollen clothes, socks, tuque, sweater and burgundy corduroy pants, all of which made it unnecessary to lie under the foul-smelling blankets during the day.

On sunny days, when the earth shone more than the sky, I would go out into the garden, which was buried under nearly a metre of snow. The roads were so snow covered that you could see only footprints and pawprints, but no paths. I couldn't find a shovel to dig my way to the end of the yard to go to the outhouse or the well. The long icicles that hung from the eaves encircling the house looked like pearls adorning a princess's headband.

This rather imposing landscape, stretched out before my eyes the entire day as I looked out the window, made me stop thinking about the Marie and Petre story. During the harsh winter, a prisoner of the snow, wind, and frost, I constructed a sunny story redolent of oranges, a story that would unfold on the shores of Asia Minor. The Trojan War was about to break out in my mind. I had awoken to an apocalyptic atmosphere, just as the legendary civilization was being threatened by the Greeks. The battle had not begun, walls were not yet tumbling down, and the violent Greek warriors had not yet appeared on the scene.

I was one of Priam's many daughters, but not Cassandra. I wanted to be any one of the other girls, perhaps the one named Zenaida.

For the last time, I eagerly looked at my parents, brothers, sisters, sisters-in-law, brothers-in-law, servants, teachers, actors, and dancers, before watching them all die. I wandered through the secret corners, elaborately decorated rooms, bedrooms, and bathrooms of the citadel before losing them for ever. Peering out of the slits along the ramparts, I could follow brave Achilles, for whom I was the vulnerable heel. Surrounded by hordes of mercenaries, facing troops of foot soldiers, he looked up, surveying the narrow windows, suspecting my terrified presence behind them. He impatiently awaited the fall of the city. Achilles always remained close to the great iron gate that still separated the two civilizations, so that he would be among the first to enter and face all the danger. He knew that he had to be the first one to see me, to touch me, to snatch me from the others. In that way, he could both save and capture me. He would become my saviour, but also my master. He would have to protect me from the violence, savagery, brutality, and rape of the soldiers.

Achilles still had the scent of our previous encounter, which had occurred at a time when the two cities had not yet broken off their friendly relations with one another.

One scorching day, his ship had docked on the shores of Asia Minor. My father greeted his ambassador with characteristic Eastern hospitality and courtesy. He knew how risky it was to have such relations with foreigners who only came to Troy to spy on its people. However, Prince Priam, my prolific father, had put Achilles up in the centre of our home and allowed him to go anywhere. He had introduced the Greek to our extended family, in which the ties among relatives and the names of aunts, uncles, cousins, and spouses were enough to make outsiders dizzy. I served as his guide to the labyrinth of Troy. My father had not assigned a guard to watch out for me, nor had he ordered any surveillance, although he knew how much Achilles, the son of the Greek king Peleus, liked me, and even loved me. He knew that the best defence against the man dressed in animal hide that was barely tanned and who knew little about soap, perfume, and essential oils, was my confidence and pride as an educated young woman, dressed in silk, who had been nourished on the sweet fruits of the oasis.

My ankles were garlanded with strings of real pearls, while he ate raw meat with his dirty and unmanicured hands. Priam had nothing to fear. Humbled by so much kindness and refinement, the guest was pitiable enough to arouse my father's compassion. Achilles still remembered a world in which boys had to be courteous, in which girls were so clever that they needed no protectors. Girls rode alongside men, they were educated and brought up to respect knowledge and frequent libraries, and they wore indecent clothing that revealed their arms, necks, and sometimes their breasts. They knew how to make do with very little during long caravan trips across the desert, but they also appreciated the fine food of imperial feasts. Women had the freedom to choose their partners. They learned to read and write, and, on hot summer days, they would retire to the shade of the library, accompanied by their tutors and nurses.

Achilles was going to make Zenaida his slave. He would draw lots for her and win her as part of the spoils of war. Then, to make up for the contempt with which he had been treated in the past, he was going to make her swab the deck of the ship all the way to Greece, force her to sleep in the crowded hold, and feed her cheese and dried meat. In Achilles's cold country, Zenaida would trade her diaphanous clothes, which were light and almost transparent, for clothes in dreary colours made of rough, coarse fabric. She would give up the life of a princess forever. Out of jealousy, he would lock her up in the house, close to the servants. Instead of enjoying books, having the pleasure of touching the grainy surface of parchment scrolls, and beholding the dried leather manuscripts held in libraries, she would spend the rest of her days behind a loom or in front of a smoky hearth counting warp threads with a blunt needle. The only company she would keep would be ignorant slaves or brutal and dirty manservants. In the evening, the arrival of her starving and exhausted husband might be cause for some happiness. But, in fact, it would just bring more suffering or additional work. Once the household was asleep, she would have to endure perfunctory and miserable sex, after which she would spend the long winter's night awake, disturbed by the noisy sleep of her snoring husband.

All of this made me weep. I saw myself already imprisoned, in chains, nailed to the deck of the ship, looking out at the ruins and remains of the walls still smoking from the fire that had consumed them. The citadel of Troy was behind us. I had been driven out of the land of women forever. Now I would be forcibly living in a distant exile, leading a cursed life in the land of cheese. Achilles was trying to conquer his fears through violence. But his efforts to conquer me would not work. His attempts at seduction made him seem even more ridiculous. We were irremediably separated. It was not worth trying because Zenaida would not even tolerate having an animal come close to her. She preferred to share her life with the prisoners, who were locked up and thrown into the bottom of the boat, who were hot, thirsty, and prostrated by their wounds. It was the only chance to make what had just disappeared survive. Another war was beginning here.

This time, my story was governed by stricter rules, as opposed to the liberties that could be taken in Marie's case. Restricting the scene of the action to the cabins, deck, and hold of a ship, I had to follow other paths. I had to sacrifice actions to concentrate on details. Unfortunately, Zenaida did not have the same freedom of movement as Marie, at least not before she arrived in Greece. I wanted to hang on to this piece of the story at all costs. Reliving the pain of my marvellous princess was true therapy for me. With each stroke of the oars propelling the ship onward, I was taken farther and farther from the site of my happiness, from my earthly paradise. I leaned on the wooden railing for as long as I could. I surveyed the riverbanks and sun-drenched beaches, where the palms had been burned by the enraged conquerors. The Achaeans, Greek barbarians, were not content to defeat the people of Troy. They had destroyed everything, stone by stone. They had killed all the animals that they didn't consider useful or that couldn't be taken aboard; they had cut down trees and devastated the hanging gardens and terraces of orange and date trees. At the end of their swords, they had displayed the heads of little baboons that once walked along the paved city streets, with golden chains around their necks. In the ditches lay parrots whose plumage had been plucked. I now saw parrot feathers adorning the hats made of untreated sheepskin, which the Greeks wore.

The soldiers had not bound the women prisoners up in chains because they knew that no one would be tempted to return to the smoking ruins. Even during the darkest disasters, they were capable of living in hope and nourishing their souls with thoughts of the future.

During the funeral march toward the ship, our guards did not allow us to examine the mutilated corpses. This left us with the hope that our heroes, our brave knights, were not all dead. Deep down in our souls we clung to the possibility that one day the city of Troy would be reborn; otherwise, would we have agreed to the torture of exile and prison? Would all the beautiful princesses, descendants of imperial families, have accepted the barbaric violence and domination of the Greeks?

As for me, how could I let Achilles penetrate the sacred depths of my body, instead of letting him drown in his own blood or making him writhe in agony, after exposing his entrails to the poison I carried in tiny capsules hidden in the most intimate cavities of my body.

I had decided to begin my Greek story with the moment when I was near Achilles. That's why I spared his life. Paris had shot his poisoned arrow. But during the battle my hero was wearing a pair of leather boots, the ankles of which were bronze coated. And, besides, who else among the Greeks could I use? Agamemnon, next to my dear Cassandra, my poor sister, was heading back home, to his death, to join Clytemnestra who awaited him with the red carpet of temptation, while Ulysses was preparing for his long odyssey. Achilles seemed perfect for my story. He was handsome, valiant, courageous, strong, impulsive, rough, and rather stupid. He would be ideal as my potential prey. Achilles was sensitive enough to fall madly in love with Zenaida, yet proud enough to rebel against her contempt and indifference.

For Achilles-Petre, the infernal torture of love had begun, to which there was no obvious barrier except the curse and bewildering opposition of the woman. It would have been so simple if Zenaida had been a docile prisoner, grateful for the fact that the roulette wheel of life—actually rigged by Achilles—had destined her for a prince rather than a married sailor with ten children. The Trojan War had taken place. Achilles loved her. Everything was in place for a beautiful love story.

During the long voyage back, Zenaida insisted on being treated like a slave. Achilles took her into his cabin to use for his personal pleasure as often as he liked, after which he had to let her go back down to join the other princesses, huddled like a flock of scruffy birds in the stinking hold of the ship, tossed about by an increasingly turbulent sea.

It was quite a difficult story for me. I was happy that there was no one to disturb me. Any human company might have been a burden, a disquieting obstacle to my storytelling process. Every second was precious. There were moments when I tortured myself looking for the most fitting and appropriate details, the most tragic colours, and the saddest music. I thought about everything, even about smells, and went on to choose the most unbearable odours.

The most awkward part for me was that I had to eat, get washed, relieve myself, go out to get fresh air, and stretch my legs. Yet, even when I was doing all that, I was still Zenaida. The poverty that surrounded me was the poverty of slaves. Just like the case of the prisoner banished from her empire, my situation was pitiful and hopeless.

Outside, terrible winds began to blow, winds that I would need upon arrival in my new country, where the coastline was exposed to tempests and icy storms. Greece had a climate that was far too mild for my story; Achilles's country, therefore, had to be relocated a little higher, to the north-west.

My distance from Achilles and Zenaida made the events they were experiencing rather difficult, almost unbelievable. These events seemed as implausible to me as the good things coming in my life. I could not invest my soul in them, just as I could not believe in salvation, individual progress, or family. The existence of these events was just as impossible as the existence of happiness. They were all mere fantasies, for as soon as I opened my eyes, there was nothing left in the empty bedroom except spiders, which had begun to spin their webs in the corners and on the crumbling walls.

George came to see me at the end of the month.

What were we going to do with the child? My nausea was not as devastating as the previous time. I was already accustomed to carrying this burden in my woman's body. It was my true nature, which I had been suppressing in the last while.

In the usual, normal course of life, I was opposed to being a sterile intellectual. I was made to procreate. I was at peace, while George worried about my health. What would be the consequences of a pregnancy that occurred so soon after an abortion?

But … good God! No, it couldn't be true! Was he was seriously thinking of keeping the baby?

January

To prolong the happiness of having produced this fruit with our filthy bodies, I kept the child for another month. We knew that it was impossible to wait very long, but we delayed the abortion for as long as we could, knowing we would be devastated by sadness. The only proof we had of our sin was my swollen breasts, the particular scent of my body, and the crazed and constant desire of the man whose woman, whose wife, I had become.

George was not as awkward as he had been when he first began to visit me. During our brief encounters, he had become the only certainty in my life. He would sit at the edge of the bed, near me, and take my hand. Every time I closed my eyes, trying to fall asleep, he would shake me hard. I had never told him the stories of Marie and Petre, nor of Zenaida and Achilles. He felt their presence, however. He read these stories in the twitching of my eyelids, the quivering of my lips, and the wrinkling of my brow. I no longer noticed his lined face or white hair. In my eyes, he was the same boy I had once been so fond of and with whom I had parted sixteen years earlier. What more could I want?

I awoke in January without having been aware of the winter holidays. What a fantastic lie they are: if people didn't exist, the holidays wouldn't exist either. There had been no breath of air and no aroma signalling the coming of Christmas. There had been no Star of Bethlehem in the sky, no scent of myrrh and frankincense, no newborn crying. I was not aware that it was New Year's until George came over, bearing wine, pastries, and oranges.

One Monday morning, when it was bitterly cold, I went to Craiova with George. We could no longer postpone the abortion without endangering my health. We went back to the same hospital, to the same doctor, who joked as he examined me. I felt the same hand of the same nurse on my mouth. The little embryo fell into the same kidney-shaped metal dish with chipped enamel. I lay down on my stomach in the same recovery room. The only thing that was different was the deep and infinite tenderness with which George protected me. He stayed at my bedside and gently stroked my neck with two fingers. With his other hand, he affectionately squeezed my palm against his knees. He was crying silently, trying to suppress the sound of his sobs and stop the flow of tears.

When we got to George's house this time, his wife was not as welcoming as she had been in November. From the beginning, she had gathered that I was carrying her husband's child in my belly, and so she didn't have any sympathy for our anguish. Hers was much greater when she saw how carefully her husband took care of me and shielded me from her anger and hatred. She cried, screamed, and cursed me, while I sat politely on the edge of the couch, my hands folded in my lap and my head bowed. George gave me looks suggesting I not listen to her, not pay attention to one single thing she was saying. We were both silent amidst an avalanche of bad words.

At night, I slept in the living room, on the couch. George and his wife argued for several hours in their bedroom. But I fell asleep before their quarrel had ended.

I woke up feeling a cold hand on my forehead. It was George. He was asking me if I was in pain. No, I thought everything was alright, although I had a fever. I got up to go to the bathroom and at that moment was gripped by unbearable abdominal pain. George wanted to call an ambulance. Perhaps I should go to the hospital. From the bedroom, his wife shouted that it wasn't anything serious. It was normal to have pain after repeated abortions.

George took me home in a taxi, which he had paid for, and then took the cab right back to Craiova. He had to work the following day.

Once again, I recovered quickly. I had little discomfort, little bleeding, little fever. Almost nothing, in fact.

At the end of the month, Mihai came to see me. The layer of snow had shrunk and he had been able to drive right into the yard. He brought me food, mainly canned food and biscuits. For the voyage, he said. Was he joking? Yes, of course. This story was really funny. He had made a bet that I would come back from the seashore. He asked how much longer I was going to sail the seas. Hadn't I had enough of my desert island?

When I had left eight months earlier, Mihai had noticed the books I was taking with me. Like me, his first inclination was to consider everything an adventure. However, he hadn't said anything to me. Now, perhaps, he was having fun with his friends at my expense.

Daniel was still in Buzau. He had grown used to my cousin's two daughters and didn't seem to miss his mother. He had forgotten all about me.

There was nothing more between Mihai and me than there had been before we were separated. After we spent a few hours together, it was as if we had only been apart for a day. I even had the impression that he had faint erotic feelings for me. Who knows? If I hadn't still been bleeding, I might have possibly given in to him. I had become incapable of refusing such advances, no matter where they came from. Since yearning for matriarchy, I no longer had the ability to choose men. Turning him down made him distant again. He took it as revenge and thought that I was angry with him. It didn't matter. The more we spoke, the less close we were and the colder our relationship grew.

He left before sundown.

We both understood that it would be impossible to resume our life as a couple, particularly since there wasn't even an ounce of love left between us. But that wasn't all. The fact that we had experienced our disenchantment separately and silently had forever undermined our marriage. Without tears, without reproach, everything had just grown irrevocably cold.

February

I had spent the first half of January alone again. My tongue had swollen between my teeth. The slightest contact with my gingivitis-stricken gums or my decaying molars filled me with disgust. I could already feel my physical decay, through my mouth, where I had begun to get a taste of my rotting flesh. This small orifice was no longer the privileged space for kissing or eating, but rather the mouth of a sewer through which flowed a miasma of acids and digestive juices that were breaking down.

Also, just as I was becoming accustomed to the hum of the radio, to the outdated tunes that I had learned to seek out across all the stations, the machine died. For the first time, I was frightened by the silence that invaded the bedroom so suddenly. I would sometimes be awakened shortly after midnight by the vibration of the windows, when the wind changed direction. How had the old women in the area been able to sleep all this time without dying of terror?

The weather was gradually warming up. Every new day, the snowbanks shrank by a few centimetres. Mud, however, made the paths completely impassable. By the end of February, all this mud and water would spill out of the overflowing ditches and lie everywhere.

I didn't try to leave the yard or walk out into the street. I walked from one door to another along the cement path, wearing a pair of worn running shoes. I had better clothing now. I got the small amount of water I needed from the drain spout. That had been my son's discovery. I filtered it using a cotton handkerchief and added a bit of sugar.

My ancestors' life together had become fraught with danger. Marie had needed a long convalescence to recover from her broken bones and bruised arms. She was just hanging on, on the brink of survival because her husband's hatred had reached its peak. Her only refuge was her little shack, which the stranger still didn't dare to enter, kept at bay by superstitions and primeval fears. Her house was like a fortress and Marie had barricaded herself inside during the winter. Her only link to the outside world, to the village, which was also hibernating, was her older sister Stana. She was the one who brought her the few items she needed from the store. Petre didn't have the courage to react to this boycott. And I, cruel person that I was, couldn't decide to give up the fight and accept the idea of a mediocre marriage: a house, with an orchard out front, a mother and father, children, a cart and two horses. Wasn't it too simple to live like that?

Marie's existence was as bleak as mine. From her window she could see the same trees as I could, now stripped of their leaves and covered in frost, the same earth mixed with leaves and straw, and the same gloomy sky. Like me, she shivered in the cold and ate very little. She was also devoid of feelings and desires. During this time, the man—my poor great-grandfather—was still madly in love with her. I was determined to preserve the difference between the two of them, to elevate Marie above this love, to make her indifferent to the advances of my ancestor, who, as Aunt Cecilia would have it, was a rather good-looking and virile young man. But that was not part of my story. I insisted on making Marie blind to all masculine charms.

After a beautiful week of sunshine, the weather turned bad once again. The village was buried in deep snow, which was blown in by icy, bitter winds directly from the steppes of Russia. George came to see me despite the harsh conditions. Generous old George. I was so grateful to him for seeking me out, for scouring the ruins to find me. What was driving him to come to me with his arms full of the most exquisite and exotic fruit, which had such a perfect shape and colour that they looked like fake plastic fruit? Fruit was so expensive at this time of year that, like a rude peasant, I didn't hesitate to tell him that he should have brought me apples instead. But George was so kind that he didn't take any of my sarcastic comments seriously. He pulled a small television set out of his vinyl suitcase and immediately turned it on. He had saved for last an item he thought I would be most pleased with: a brand-new electric coffee maker. He had noticed that my little coffee pot and immersion heater required too much fussing, even for someone as sinfully fond of coffee as I was. This time, he also brought twenty baguettes, pickled fish, and smoked cheese. Carrying this load of provisions in a backpack and two small suitcases, over a distance of three kilometres, had made him sweat profusely.

Later, after I had eaten enough and looked at an orange for a long time, I asked about his wife. How was she reacting to all this?

She had left him and had moved back in with her parents. Not because of my abortion but because of his behaviour afterward. Because of the way he had looked after me, the way he cared for me and worried about me, and the trips he was preparing to make to the village in such bad weather, she no longer had any doubts. Although he tried his best to placate her, George had nonetheless decided to stay with me. I was the chosen one, I had won without lifting a finger. His wife had decided to leave him for the time being, without splitting their possessions or taking any kind of legal action yet.

Did he love me? Yes, he loved me tremendously. He didn't have the words to tell me how much, and how grateful he was for the chance to love me openly, even so late in life. His friendship and affection during our childhood had never been innocent, like mine. If he hadn't been so shy, he might have found a way to show me how much he desired me, how happy he would have been with me, and how much my departure had left him with a sadness he would never get over.

George was a modern-day version of my beloved Achilles. But how could I be happy about this conquest? The world was so unbearable without heroes, without glorious events like wars. My uncles had really been right to look down on the weak and feeble. It was natural for men to fight each other, to be in a constant battle for everything, to flex their muscles before the ritual of mating. They went to war and lived in a permanent state of violence, blood, and death.

George would ask me whether I was happy.

But how could you be happy when you came from the land of cheese? If the value of everything was based on the value of cheese and if everything smelled of cheese? How could you be happy if there wasn't the slightest chance, the slightest possibility of eluding your miserable condition? How could you not miss those few infinitesimal moments of escape, those incursions into the villas of the late Renaissance? I had seen so much beauty in the parallel lives into which I had peered that it was normal, in the depths of despair, to be afraid of finding myself in a dilapidated room.

Unlike me, George was not at all interested in obsessing about his origins, whereas this complex had tormented me from the very beginning. Everyone comes from somewhere; everyone is born somewhere. Why was that so important? Was it really that meaningful?

Yes. For me, origin was really important. I didn't want to come from here. I didn't want to have the parents that I had. I didn't want my past to smell of alcohol and cheese. I didn't want to have wasted my life, for nothing.

I was deeply sorry that I had been forced to admit it. A certain modesty, which I had inherited from my predecessors, had kept me from confessing how much I loved this solitude, how much I enjoyed the absence of other people. How happy I was to have no ancestors. When my parents died, I had felt only fleeting pangs of pity, but no regret. As long as they were alive, they remained my guardians, even at a distance. The force with which they held me back could only be offset by their physical disappearance. The death of my parents had been an enormous relief for me. It had been the sole possibility, the only chance of earning a better place in the sun.

I was not concerned as I observed the wrinkles under my eyes growing deeper day by day. I calmly observed my body deteriorating: my hair grew thinner and lost its colour, my belly was already like a wet sponge. There were a few stiff hairs under my chin, my nipples drooped, flabby bulges appeared. For me, age was the only true victory. I just wanted to grow old more quickly. If my body shrank, if the skin on my face became scaly, then perhaps everything about my life would change as well. I could no longer live with such a burden.

Did I want George to bring me books?

Books? What a strange idea! What good would they do? Didn't I already have proof that you could live just as well without them, without reading a single line of writing? Without books and without all the things that people desperately cling to.

Did I need any other examples, other than the lives of my parents, to come to the conclusion that my life, like everyone else's life, in fact, began with ignorance and ended with resignation? That love, sadness, and despair are the same everywhere.

Toward the end of the month, there were a few days of good weather. The sun shone almost all day, warming the frigid winter air a bit.

I took advantage of the milder temperatures to go to the well and bring home a pail of fresh water. I had enough strength now to be able to turn the heavy, rusty wheel. The wooden bucket was covered with moss and had begun to rot. Yet, the taste of pure water, after the mineral, sandy soup I had been drinking all winter, seemed extraordinary to me. I filled the coffee maker with water, brewed some coffee, and then gulped down three large cups full. The pleasant aroma, which I had longed for so much and almost dreamed about, filled the room and lifted my spirits. For no reason, I found myself cheerful once more.

A cup of coffee, however, immediately triggers a nervous reaction, a thought, an idea in which you must invest passionately. That was how the coffee led to television. Unfortunately, my TV only picked up the national channel, which preyed on a people kept in the dark. In addition to the devastating disasters of summer and winter—droughts, rainstorms, snowstorms, and floods—television was a permanent catastrophe. As effective as biological weapons, television worked day and night, the whole year long, regardless of the season. Previously, I would never have had the patience to watch such programs, from the first to the last episode. Now, after having been subjected to this treatment, I watched my despair, my helplessness, my rage, and my loneliness at night, before going to sleep. I realized that my blood pressure had gone up, that my blood was not circulating normally through my body, forgetting, lazily, to flow to my fingertips, that my hips were covered in sores. I found the programs of a political nature, soap operas, investigative reports on social issues in Moldavia, petty and confusing. They upset the neurons in my brain, which had lost its ability to think and discern what was real. It would have been much easier for me to re-establish contact with the outside world had television not existed.

The aroma of coffee, paired with sunshine, introduced a bit of excitement into my life, along with a certain taste for cleanliness and a faint desire for action. Finally, after six months of confinement in my bedroom, I opened the window. A damp, cool, and prophetic wind blew in from the river, whose banks were overflowing.

But the moments of euphoria, of serenity before the coming of spring, quickly disappeared. I wanted to break with everything that was behind me. Who could yearn for a world that valued the exuberant bingo caller on the TV game show, the six-o'clock news anchor with her big, sensual, blood-red lips, along with entertaining Saturday night shows and frivolous ones broadcast on Sunday afternoons?

On the last Saturday of the month, a red car stopped in front of the main gate. The horn honked loudly and woke me up from my morning sleep. I opened the window and saw George coming up the driveway with his arms full of books, taking care not to slip in the mud. It was his car, an old Ford, which he used only very rarely. He never drove to the village because it was too costly and because the roads were in poor shape. In Craiova, he always parked the car in a friend's yard, under a makeshift shelter.

George was making his library available to me. Not all at once, but bit by bit. The books belonged to his wife; she had bought them when she lived with her parents, who were Jewish. She was meticulous and quite well educated, and had organized the library according to collections, priorities, and recent books. But she had never been in a hurry to read them. George wasn't particularly interested in reading them either. From time to time, he would leaf through a book that had an especially attractive cover. So, the extensive library had collected dust in their apartment, forgotten and neglected by its owners. When she left, his wife had shown no interest in taking her own books. They had remained in George's possession, therefore, as if he reigned over an indefinable empire: was this a victory or a disaster?

He began by bringing me the contents of the top shelf, attached to the ceiling, which he reached by standing on a ladder. The first shipment contained about three metres of books. He had retained the way his in-laws had calculated the value of their daughter's dowry. We made an inventory of the books as if they were toys. After all these years, George was finally becoming familiar with his own library. He looked at the plump tomes as I had done when surveying the nearby ruins and dilapidated houses a year earlier. No emotion, no pleasure, just slight curiosity.

The top shelf had housed the collection of "Complete Works," which included excessively thick books with white covers and black titles, like tombs in which the authors found death over and over, and forever more. His wife had purchased everything that was recommended to her, without making any personal choices.

George went back home on Sunday evening, leaving me with a new form of entertainment. Even if I didn't read the books, he said, I could still enjoy myself by leafing through them.

May

I woke up abruptly in the middle of spring.

I had spent two months reading the books that George had brought me. During that time, I was hardly aware that the deep snow had melted; I had taken little notice of the fierce winds, the storms that came up at the end of March, and the cold rain tinted blue by the thick fogs of April. I hadn't seen the birds return, the short-lived snowdrops bloom, or the trees turn green. I had barricaded myself in the house, behind piles of books, hundreds of yellowed books with brittle pages, covers disfigured by insects, and title pages scarred by dedications. The most intimate, the most vivid, was one I found at the beginning of the Zaslavsky serials, written in pencil and misspelled: "Received from my deer husband. Topala Florika, March 1952."

I had begun with Maiorescu. After reading three weighty tomes that included all the philosopher's juvenilia, I played a sort of Russian roulette with the authors who occupied my bedroom. I looked at the wise writers from a distance, their books all piled up against the wall, the spines of which were turned toward me. I pointed my finger and said, "You!"

The most boring of all were the eight volumes containing the complete works of Shakespeare. I wasted ten whole days on them. It took me two days to understand the words, "A horse, a horse! My kingdom for a horse!"

and another whole day to decipher "Now is the winter of our discontent made glorious summer by this sun of York." The reason being that the play from which these quotations are taken, *Richard III*, was hidden in volume one, which I tended to skip every time I settled in to read Shakespeare. Even worse, because I was distracted, I also skipped the first couplet. I even thought that I had stumbled upon an alternate translation. I read almost all the plays looking for Roseline and Bottom. Then I looked at all of those that featured twins.

With Goethe, however, things got a bit more complicated. Who would have thought that I would like *Faust*? I didn't expect to, and, in any case, I didn't want to read all of it. The long poem surprised me because all I had known about *Faust* was something about Mephistopheles and Margarete's final embrace. But what about Helena, the homunculus in his glass vial, the cohorts of angels, philosophers and Greek heroes, kings, noblemen, and the Walpurgis nights? What were they all doing there? For thirty years, I had been convinced that Faust would die of happiness. Beware of pleasure, for it is the work of the devil, that's what I knew about it. It was too late to find out that it was definitely Mephisto who was the unhappy character in the book.

I quickly skimmed over the authors who kept their distance, and then got to Beckett, the first revelation in the library that I was browsing through out of sense of obligation toward George. I was fortunate enough to understand every word of *Molloy*. I was amused by Camier's reactions to his chance encounters at the train station. Few things in this world are as beautiful as the beginning of *Mercier and Camier*, Moran's relations with his son, or the ending of *Molloy*, with its description of the swarm of bees that turn into a little dust of annulets and wings.

Among the collection of complete works, I set aside the *Odyssey* and the *Iliad*. I knew that once I had read them, my own story would be enriched with new faces and new adventures. Even though I had not pursued the story of Zenaida and Achilles since the winter, the two had kept on conducting their silent battle on the deck of the ship that was carrying them back to Hellas.

The following pile contained 103 books in a collection called "World Literature." The books had greenish covers with elaborate arabesque designs and titles inscribed in green letters on a square in the centre. The pages were yellow and rather thick, and the type was set in large characters, as clear as a mirror.

Of Diderot's works, I selected *Paradox of the Actor*, *Salons*, and his *Essay on Painting*, despite his premise that there were plenty of artists who could draw well, but few good colourists.

I also delved into Torquato Tasso, whose life was more thrilling than his writing. Unlike Ariosto, Tasso got into trouble for expressing his opinions. His patron Alfonso II d'Este had him committed to an insane asylum for seven years. It has been said, however, that the real reason behind Tasso's mental illness was his love for the duke's sister, Leonora. Goethe said as much in a play he wrote.

An inscription on the cover of a work by Giacomo Leopardi caught my attention: "A Classicist among the Romantics." In *Small Moral Works*, Leopardi rejects the Romantic exaltation that was inflaming the minds of his contemporaries. He was also presumed to be sceptical because of his infirmity. Nevertheless, I liked the fact that Leopardi made an effort to believe in the perfectibility of mankind. He discovered rather late that it was possible for happiness to come when you stop contradicting the truths put forward in your time.

I appreciated the beginning of Virgil's work. I liked its simplicity, especially because there were features in it that could enhance my own story. After reading his work, I understood that my Zenaida's hope was Aeneas, her second cousin and husband of Creusa. Aeneas was the only one who had escaped after the war and fled beyond the crumbling walls of Troy. I couldn't include him in my dreams, however. For me, the existence of that Creusa, the wife of Aeneas, was not right, since she had been abandoned at the edge of the city. But what was particularly intolerable was the self-immolation of the distraught Dido, who took her life for the love of Aeneas. Hector's unfortunate wife Andromache, on the other hand, gave me new ideas, especially since she had become Pyrrhus's slave after the fall of Troy.

Turning to the Spanish novel, I moved on to volumes from the 1960s. The covers were much plainer. They had a black border with the title and the author's name written in tall, narrow letters. At the bottom of the cover was the image of a globe, divided into meridians, placed next to an open book. Cervantes's *Exemplary Novels* was illustrated with two paintings by Velázquez, *Breakfast* on the front cover and *Old Woman Frying Eggs* on the back cover. *Guzmán de Alfarache* by Mateo Alemán had a picture of Velázquez's *The Triumph of Bacchus* on the cover.

Spanish tramps appealed to me much more than the ones who populated Beckett's works. They were cheerful, optimistic, and, in general, willing to learn something from their adventures. I was enchanted by the novels of

Cervantes because of the unsystematic, chaotic movement of the heroes, and by the way in which they evoked the past for the sheer love of storytelling. Novels provided answers to questions that no one asked anymore. That's why I found *The Travails of Persiles and Sigismunda* much more effective than any book of philosophy. I found the prologue particularly charming because it was the only opportunity to get a glimpse into the author's true self. By breaking the rules of propriety, he was the first to have touched me, and that honoured me. On the title page of the book by Mateo Alemán, I found the censor's authorization for the book to be published and the extraordinary observation that plebians always have friends of low quality. His protagonist, Guzmán the Jew, was another person obsessed by his origins.

I then moved on to the English novel, to the pen-and-ink writers of the eighteenth-century. It was the pen that explained their infinite patience: they would never tire of supplying details or going over what they had already said a thousand times before.

I read *The History of Pendennis* by Thackeray and *Ernest Pontifex or The Way of All Flesh* by Samuel Butler. I especially liked the way they describe the minor flaws that transform their heroes into monsters. The English mastered the science of writing about qualities that were cultivated to excess. That's why I had so much sympathy for Ernest's Aunt Alethea, who often said, "Nothing is well done nor worth doing unless, take it all round, it has come pretty easily."

English writers were also in the habit of publishing pamphlets. Tobias Smollett, known for *The Adventures of Roderick Random*, and Henry Fielding, author of *Joseph Andrews*, are good examples. We read about the innocent Joseph who experiences so much trouble simply because he is the brother of Pamela, whose virtues only cause him problems.

But why were the English so well represented? I was reviving the preferences and tastes of a man I didn't know anything about. It was clear that the former owner of the library had had boundless patience. Or perhaps the person who had possessed this empire was an infirm child whose parents had tried to help him tolerate his lack of mobility.

One Sunday morning, I had the most delightful encounter with Stendhal. I found the definition he gave of egotism in *The Life of Henry Brulard* and *Memoirs of an Egotist* very enlightening. The pages were covered in hand-drawn sketches. Stendhal had drawn all the rooms of all the cities he had seen, as well as the streets he had walked along where something essential had happened in his life. All that to counter the terrible realization that facts never truly match our feelings. He convinced me, sadly, that no one can ever change substantially. At the age of fifty, all of us retain the same obsessions and the same fears we had when we were eighteen.

It was snowing. Once again, the branches of the apple tree were laden with snow that would begin to melt the next day. I liked water that came from snow better than rainwater and was sorry that I couldn't keep it longer.

Strindberg continued to offer the warmest description of a cold world.

I got bogged down in Novalis, however. What really got on my nerves was his tendency to delve into the dreams of other people. I didn't like Novalis's way of immersing himself in the Orient. His fantasies didn't match my own in any way.

I read the Poe stories that had inspired mid-twentieth-century American horror films, with Gothic castles and ghosts. America had cultivated its tastes for the occult too early.

It was such a pleasure to discover the Greek world of *Daphnis and Chloe*, to immerse myself in the life of Lesbos and the changing of the seasons.

I loved *Gora* by Tagore, the foot soldier of Hinduism, who believed that any religion emptied of its content and reduced to ritual can lead to extremism.

Poor books. They had become a burden, a punishment. What a sad fate! But the part of my new activity that irritated me the most, dilettante that I was, was that they restricted my own stories and sapped them of their living content. The more I read, the weaker and more tedious my hero's exploits became. Unwittingly, I noticed that too many aspects of my own stories were unrealistic. I needed to include many more details, such as the condition of Oriental women. My Zenaida could not be forever nostalgic for Priam's castle, nor the library, to which women did not even have access, nor journeys by caravan across the desert, nor indecent nudity. Life in Hellas, on the other hand, was less dire than I was making it out to be.

Christopher Marlowe was the most helpful to me. *Tamburlaine the Great* offered the most beautiful spectacle. In this world, there is no greater love scene than the one between Zenocrate, Tamburlaine, and Agydas. Agydas, who is in love with Zenocrate, an Egyptian princess, tries to plant the seeds of rebellion in her soul and incite hatred for the Scythian bandit Tamburlaine, who holds her captive as his concubine, rather than wife. But Zenocrate declares her undying fidelity to Tamburlaine. Tamburlaine approaches, takes the woman's hand, and exits, all the while staring at Agydas. I was moved by the beginning of their relationship. I really loved it. The barbarian of Scythia captures the beautiful Zenocrate, steals her treasures, but he also falls madly in love with her. Subsequent events, however, are not part of my story. Zenocrate becomes a slave, Tamburlaine's love slave, and she gives him sons, following him across the steppes of Asia. She never asks for anything. Caught between her father and her lover, who continue to fight one another, she is the most beautiful woman ever.

In Théophile Gauthier's *Arria Marcella*, I was struck by the discussion of Solomon's famous dictum:

"There is nothing new under the sun," replied Fabio; "and the aphorism itself is not new, inasmuch as it was formulated by Solomon."

"Perhaps there may be something new under the moon," observed Octavian, with a smile of melancholy irony.

In Mark Twain, simple people were always the ones who experienced the most extraordinary adventures. I liked that. Twain's Yankee engineer, the son of a blacksmith who is "nearly barren of sentiment," is transported back in time to the court of King Arthur.

In Bulat Okudzhava's book *Dilettantes' Travels*, I was interested in what the author had to say about travellers, although I'm not sure why. Even dilettantes travel, he says. Even those who ultimately forget what they see, even those who are not fully prepared for their adventures, want to set out on journeys. Having the courage to leave home is what really matters.

At the end of April, I found myself reading *The Stone Raft* by José Saramago, in which I noted a sentence in Romanian, "Si noi sîntem iberici," which translates as "We are also Iberians."

Looking out my window one day, I was stunned to see how green the garden was. Buds had long since burst open and the treetops were already crowned with white flowers. Every day the sun left the village blanketed in a light coat of mist because the earth still bore the chill of winter. The scents of the season wafted up in the moist air, not yet laden with dust. The breeze also swept up pollen, smoke, violet petals, and the silt left behind by the floods. Everything was laid out in front of me: damp wood, black mud, rusty doors, a dirty driveway, my godmother's house with its slightly truncated map of Australia, bare trees on one side, green ones on the other. Everything exuded the odour of awakening. Awakening from a nightmare. Every gust of wind, every drop of rain was proof that we were all alive. We were not dead. A complete waste, actually, but we were alive.

It was probably May. I didn't know the exact date. From George's comings and goings, I could only keep track of the days of the week. It was on a Wednesday that I realized that a year had passed since I had come here. George had been gone for two days and would be back in three more. That's all I knew, that's all I had known for a very long time.

I left the pile of books in the middle of the room and went out for a walk along the deserted roads. I put on warm clothing and the rubber boots that George had brought, and without which life would be unimaginable in this place.

I could hear the cry of the cuckoo coming from the big well. The cuckoo, a solitary bird, had always been impossible to locate. I stopped in my tracks and looked all around. Seven turtledoves were perched on the electric wires, looking like pearls strung together on a necklace.

My entire childhood came back to me suddenly and relentlessly. My soul was not filled with images or memories, not with sounds or odours either. And yet, I knew, at that moment, that I was feeling my childhood. Everything that was essential to me was there. Nothing else had happened during my months of reading.

So what? What could I do? Why stay? Why go back? I no longer had anyone, anywhere. No one desired me, no one was expecting me. Ileana, Mihai, Daniel? In my memory, they were just as alive or just as dead as my grandmother or Aunt Cecilia. I was bewildered and disoriented by the blurring of boundaries between what had already happened and what was yet to come. I couldn't see any reason to be either happy or sad. And that was unfortunate, just like a year earlier, when I imagined that it was the fault of my husband and his mistress.

I followed a path strewn with garbage up to the end of our vineyard. From the top of the hill, I looked down on a little stream flowing through the wide riverbed, beyond which stretched an orchard of plum trees. There was no one in the fields. The vines were all lying fallow, and should have been tended long ago, dry canes pruned, vine tendrils stretched along wires, and the weeds pulled out.

What a wasteland!

I went back into the house. I was freezing cold. It was a dreary day, and the rays of the sun hadn't penetrated the layer of clouds.

I turned the radiator on in my room and then put coffee on. I got under the covers without taking my clothes off and fell asleep. Without reliving any part of my stories. For the first time, I found them boring. They no longer seemed important to me, I no longer found them charming. I was tired of making love, of being happy, of being warm only in my dreams.

When I woke up, the feeling of being abandoned and the certainty of having nothing were just as powerful as when I had gone to sleep. I drank coffee. I looked out the window. It was warm in my room. But everything felt futile.

Three days later, I watched George come up the walk cheerfully, his arms full of new books. How could he be so pleased to see me? How could he believe that I shared his happiness? Why did he think that I would relish these worn, yellowed, tattered pages from the "Everyone's Library" collection. My God, only fools could find life so beautiful!

George, my dear friend, I am prepared to do the unforgivable. Not to kill myself, but to kill you. To cut you into small pieces, and then hide you in my cellar. I'm prepared to let the worms devour you, prepared to live each day with your stinking corpse.

Meanwhile, George was untying a package of cream cakes. He opened a bottle of cognac and poured a few drops into coffee cups. He lit two cigarettes. Finally, he smiled at me, even though I was dirty, I reeked of urine and sweat, and my hair was full of dandruff.

George, my friend, I'm going to cut you into small pieces. I'll start with your neck, with the place where your sweater rubs against your Adam's apple. And then I'll spend more time on your long, rather irritating nose, on your wrinkled cheeks, and on your excessively fat lips.

George rummaged through his last suitcase. He had brought me some deodorant spray, nicely scented soap, underwear, two new dresses, and a terry cloth bathrobe. Everything smelled so good. The clothes were so soft to the touch. Ooh! And toothpaste! Mint-flavoured toothpaste. Ah! He had also repaired the radio.

He knew perfectly well that I was dependent on objects such as these, even addicted to them. That all human beings could be tempted by them, by the charm that justified their existence. That nothing could revive a person more quickly than perfumed soap or a plush bathrobe with a monogram embroidered on the breast pocket. That this marvellous toothpaste could make you forget about your rotting body. That sadness could evaporate completely when you tried on a new dress and looked at yourself in the mirror. So much trickery and so many lies had been invented to extend our lives artificially and prevent us from dying.

June

In June, I gave up reading once and for all, although George continued to bring me new books every week. He had exhausted the thousand volumes in the "Everyone's Library" series: those with a red cover from the beginning of the collection, published a hundred years ago, and those with multicoloured covers, published after the 1950s. He had got up to the collection of art books, in what was called the "Meridian" collection, which included several hundred volumes on art history, along with dozens of art books with badly reproduced illustrations. I moved them around and changed their order so that George would not realize that I was no longer reading. The fate of the books was as dismal and useless as my own. If you didn't put everything else aside, if you didn't give up outside activities to devote yourself to them, it wasn't worth wasting your time on them. On the other hand, if you read through them in a random manner, you had no chance of finding something you would like. After so many wordy, dense, and long-winded books, after picaresque novels and thousand-page tomes by English writers, I was torn by the realization that, except for the author's name, the dimensions of the book, the colour of the covers, they all looked alike and were becoming clichéd. Taken on their own, away from the library, these poor books, like my poor stories, had no value.

Once again, I lived outside. Like all primitive creatures, I only liked the summer. Because my life depended on warm weather and its products. We primitives could only live outside. We loved to lie about in the sun and feed on the little that was available, all ready-made and free of charge. That's where my evolution stopped.

I had set the table and chair up again in the garden under the flowering apple tree. The small plot of land I had cultivated the previous year was now covered with a tangle of dried branches mixed with the offshoots of new plants. The latest war had broken out among the weeds in the garden before they invaded the surrounding woods. The vines had once again become an aggressive shrub, a scary equatorial forest full of secrets. Leaves were occupied by unknown insects that I was seeing for the first time: unicorns with branched horns; beetles with dull grey wings; June beetles; brown and hairy dung beetles; enormous bugs that looked lumpy, like tarpaper. Even the innocuous ladybug had changed, having grown bigger and more violent, flying noisily. These insects hunted and killed one another; they ate each other until the birds swooped down and snatched them out of their holes with their beaks.

The bees continued to buzz around over this brush. I wondered who the little worker bees were now working for. It was perhaps time for these pollen harvesters to finish their old task. Was there still someone in the village who kept beehives? Did the bees still travel dozens of kilometres needlessly, to extract what they needed to fill a wild comb with nectar from the flowers in my garden?

For the first time, I felt the absence of Daniel, the only one who could unravel the tangled vine tendrils intertwined with clinging weeds and branches. He was the only one who periodically destroyed the molehills and anthills.

Since the winter George had been telling me about his plan to build a new outhouse, closer to the building we occupied. I hadn't given this much thought. One Saturday, however, he launched into this difficult project. At one time, it would have been someone else's job since my parents had never been able to do this kind of dirty work. George laboured strenuously all day long. The deeper he dug, the more the earth got red and sticky, which made things harder for him. Bits of clay, which were wet and as greasy as butter, stuck to his shovel. This delayed the completion of his noble task. It was almost impossible for him to get rid of this earth, which made him change plans. Finally, he placed it in buckets and tubs, which he later emptied at the edge of the hole.

I watched him calmly. He was sweating as he dug up shovelful after shovelful of the red earth full of worms. It took me a while to realize the big change he had made. How was it possible for me to see beyond the string of buildings from the front of the house? George had torn down—I didn't know when—the wall that connected the last kitchen of the two outbuildings. Someone had dared to demolish something, in a place where things were collapsing on their own. If there was an ancestral fear anchored in each person's memory it was the fear of changing houses, beds, the place where you relieved oneself. I refused to understand how he had been capable of such an undertaking all alone. And yet, he had succeeded.

He had broken up the long chain of useless buildings, which now looked like a freight train separated from its locomotive. I didn't care where George had decided to put the toilets. He could do anything he wanted. I gave him my consent to demolish everything, so that he could set me free, so that he could help me escape the debris and hovels in which I was being held captive, in which I was suffocating.

He then asked me to help him move the old fibreboard stall, which was tipping over and which I had not been using since I arrived. Why bother, I answered. It was no use. In this new arrangement, it was even more difficult for me to go to the toilet.

"But no, it won't be more difficult. The idea is to bring the toilet closer to the bedroom," George said with a wry smile. He emphasized the word "idea," raising a finger as if to suggest that he was joking. But there was some substance to the joke, and he hoped that I would agree to the idea if possible.

He had to dismantle the stall all on his own. He moved it, piece by piece, and then rebuilt it with his own hands, adding a few more boards as well as a sheet of asbestos for the roof. On the inside wall, he nailed a toilet roll holder, on which he hung a newspaper and a women's magazine. He placed a worn piece of goat hide on the narrow toilet seat. Then he locked himself in for fifteen minutes. When he emerged, happy with how perfectly the toilet worked, he raised his index and middle fingers in a V for "victory" as if he had reached the South Pole. I pointed to the door, which didn't cover the entire frame, but he good-naturedly replied that no one was going to be watching our intimate movements in any case.

On some days, the late spring air, the brightness, and the sparkle that blanketed everything cleared the veil of smoke draped over my brain, releasing sparks, explosions, and the kind of big bang that had shaken the universe when stars, comets, and quasars were being formed or destroyed. I knew that in the darkness of my skull, in the hidden depths of its white matter, something very important was happening. But I was waking up nonetheless, watching the swarm of bees, worrying persistently about where the beehive was located. If I understood something, if there were any thoughts, they got lost in the spongy matter of my brain. Before I could classify or make sense of my ideas, they were already floating in infinite memory, with no chance of ever coming back from there. The only conscious thought I had was that having been separated and isolated from the crowd, I had perhaps escaped its faults, that I had successfully regained fundamental clarity and intelligence. I was only one step away from what I had always been looking for. I knew that my search was not directed at this place, that it had only a weak link to my arrival here. But, unfortunately, it was here that my intuition was stopping, despite my efforts to go further.

Such moments, when I found myself thinking about myself, about the person I really was, were quite rare. Each time he came, George did his best to bring me back into the fold. On the two days he spent with me, he turned the volume of the radio up full blast, knowing that the stream of words could reach me only if it they were ear-splitting. I listened to the news, to the arguments of politicians, to the complaints of voters, to talk of reform and corruption. Once again, I was under the influence of images imposed by other people, by outsiders. Little by little, I regained collective memory. George's love made me surrender, forced me to follow him, listen to him, and obey him. I realized that the time for being indifferent to others was now well behind me.

And to make the bad omen come true, one Sunday toward the end of June, I woke up surrounded by everyone. They had all gathered in my yard: George, Ilie, Ileana, Mihai, and Daniel.

George had come with tomato plants and had every intention of planting them. Ilie had come to get laid, Mihai to bring me back home. To help him do this, he had brought Daniel, who had settled in so well in Buzau that he now called my cousin "mom."

Everyone wondered who the other people were and how they were connected to me, everyone except Ileana who understood everything and got a kick out of it. She and I stayed on the sidelines watching the three men, who felt cheated and were furious about it. Ileana burst out laughing and whispered to me,

"Your place is not bad at all. Have you been having a good time?"

Who should leave and who should stay? The question kept them all immobile, paralyzed.

Which one of them had the most right to me?

The men were seated in the shade of the apple tree, around the table. Ileana and I immediately brought out glasses and plates for bread and cold cuts. George served the wine that Ilie had brought. They were talking about a small accident that Mihai had had when leaving the city of Alexandria. At a crossroads, another car had dented the right side of his car slightly.

After an hour of sitting shoulder to shoulder, Mihai decided to clarify the confusing situation, which he had decided to treat as normal, thanks to his urban upbringing and sufficiently cosmopolitan background. He came up to me and told me,

"You should start packing up your things. We are going to leave soon."

The others looked at me in silence. If they had done something else at that very moment, perhaps I would have gotten up and sat in the car right away. But the way they were all watching this spectacle made me decide to postpone the outcome. My reaction, which was worth noting, was a barely perceptible nod of the head and blink of the eye. I did not want to go with him. Not willingly, in any case. I didn't want to agree to drink my coffee on the balcony of our apartment, looking out over the houses of Rahova. I didn't want to see moths flying around our furniture either. The memory of these things returned sharply. They were killing me slowly, these things, although I hadn't realized it or suspected it earlier.

Ileana was the only one who clearly took my side. She looked at Mihai quizzically. She noted my decision, she could interpret my gestures, as subtle as they were, and regarded them as her personal victory. Throughout the years of our friendship, from the first time we met in the lobby of the university until our scaled-back and lacklustre graduation, Ileana had inculcated cynicism and rejection in me. She was five years older than me, and from the beginning had assumed the role of my spiritual master. There was no problem with this given my personality. I was a person of such little significance, so empty of content. If my former classmate didn't like me at all, it didn't bother me too much. I was her oldest friend, so to speak, and the persistence with which I kept up our relationship seemed to be a benefit to her, a small advantage.

After a certain age, it's difficult to make new friends. I had therefore become a habitual presence for her, rather like a pet cat or dog.

On that Sunday, all the feelings that had existed between us, over the years, from contempt to indifference, could be read in her smile. The fact that I failed to react convinced her that I had not changed much and that I would never change. But after so many years, she detected a hint of mischievousness in me. I was bold enough to be aggressive. Beyond the flaws of my upbringing, what drove my friend crazy was my inability to despise anyone. I could justify anything, I gave everyone the chance to stop being annoying. For Ileana, this was untenable, even unforgivable. No one deserved a second chance. Anything bad had to be nipped in the bud, without giving it a second thought.

If my marriage to Mihai was worn out, like a garment, I definitely should not waste my time looking for a way to patch it up again, trying to fix what was permanently broken. In my view, my husband was no longer worthy because he had slept with another woman. If he had been a criminal, a thief, that would have been just as serious or even less serious. The man had quite simply made a mistake, and there was no going back. In a future relationship, it would perhaps be me who would fall into the trap of infidelity. I, in turn, would have to be prepared to suffer the same consequences. Ileana's view of my marriage was just one illustration of the way she thought. For her, affection or tenderness were simply mannerisms, affectations, particularly artificial because they were frequent and obvious. In my confusion and disarray, I had met Ileana, a woman who had not invested love or friendship in our relationship, who would listen to my confidences yet poke fun at me at the same time. Nevertheless, her presence was reassuring. I had felt so comfortable listening to her scold my husband.

"What are you waiting for? Didn't you hear what she said to you? Go away! Bugger off!"

George and Ilie were thinking the same thing. But they preferred to keep their eyes glued to the bottom of their wineglasses, which they twirled around in their hands until drops of wine sprayed out. Ilie was the kind of lover who didn't come between spouses, in their marriage or in any other way. He was the type to seduce a woman easily, to get between her legs, and the next day not say hello if she happened to be with family members. He was the kind of lover who avoided former mistresses. For Ilie, it wasn't possible to be friends with a woman other than his wife after intercourse. In his view, the husband was always right. If Mihai had blamed him for everything, Ilie would not have said a word in his own defence. His peasant's wisdom was stymied by my husband's behaviour. Did Mihai really understand that I had slept with two other men? If so, how could he speak so politely to his wife instead of slapping her on both cheeks and sending her home to her mother, or else begging her to return to the marital home?

George looked like a beaten dog, ready to jump up and grab leftover bones. If I was not going back to my husband, if I did not prefer the lanky fellow with the curly hair, then perhaps I would stay with him. There was no shame or disgrace in his secondary or even third-rate position. Patience was his strength. Taking pride in having been chosen, having been preferred to so many others, was the last thing on his mind.

Except that Mihai had lost his patience. Unfortunately, he was over the quiet phase of indifference. Without looking at the others, without mentioning their presence in my house, he began to threaten me, to remind me of paperwork, unemployment, money, our apartment, our child, lawsuits—in short, everything that could turn life into a nightmare. We all listened to him in silence. Whatever they thought about his accusations, the others didn't say a word. They were helping me banish my husband from my property, from the territory that had remained foreign to him. They were already opposed to what would be considered a normal situation. They agreed with vice, they approved of it. They craved depravity and I was crowned the Queen of promiscuity.

Mihai's departure made us jubilant once again. We brought another table out of the house and got a deck of cards right away. Ilie always had a pack with him. We drank glass after glass of wine, and turned the music up as loud as it could go, breaking the silence.

When night fell, we began to dance. George only wanted me. He saw the looks that Ilie and Ileana were giving each other, and observed their carnal desire for one another. In that case, I belonged to him. And I would look stupid if I interfered with their passion.

However, I wanted Ilie, who had regained his strength as a conqueror. My husband was the only man who intimidated him and, once he was gone, Ilie had taken the place of the favourite, the man the women preferred. And what excited him the most was the attention that the new woman was paying him. But, before giving in to her own passion, my friend tried to help me. Ileana was well aware that Ilie already had a certain affection for me. So, she approached George, wrapped her arms around his skinny and shy body, and tried to lead him toward the house. Meanwhile, Ilie and I were dancing and gradually trying to make our way over to the wooden bench we had placed under the cherry tree.

Meanwhile, George had freed himself from Ileana's embrace. He came up behind us and placed his sweaty palm on my bare shoulder. With his other hand, he took Ilie's arm and gently pulled it away from me. He did his best to separate us without resentment or violence. When Ilie decided to let go, George took me in his arms and hugged me tenderly, resting his chin against my neck.

The shadow of the house fell over the garden. After a sweltering day, it was beginning to cool off.

Later, Ileana came out of the building and teetered toward us. She was drunk, but not enough to prevent her from realizing that the die was cast and that she was the winner once more.

July

July was an extremely hot month.

That's how it was in the middle of summer. It was sweltering, there was no rain and not the slightest breath of wind. July was the month when we worked the least in our village. The only difficult kind of work was harvesting tobacco leaves, which then had to be threaded onto hemp strings once they were picked. The heat softened the bittersweet glue that coated the plants, making them easier to handle. My mother and I would gather the leaves before sunrise, taking advantage of a bit of overnight humidity. In the afternoon, the entire family would sit in the shade of the old mulberry tree that stood at the main gate and we would begin to tie up the leaves. We used large, flat steel needles, which my grandfather would sharpen by striking them on an anvil. We would pull the hemp thread through the wide eye of the needle, and we would begin the process, which involved arranging the leaves back-to-back so they would dry evenly. The tip of the needle was sometimes so sharp that for days on end my fingers would be black from the cuts I got. The heavy rows of tobacco leaves were hung on the walls behind the house or on wooden frames that had been custom-built by my maternal grandfather.

This was the only chore for which my mother demanded my help. Tying up the tobacco leaves, a task that required steady attention, gave me the satisfaction of accomplishing something patiently, just like ants building an anthill.

As the air began to burn on the horizon, fruits ripened, flies and mosquitoes awoke from their long winter's sleep, and my grandparents' little shack became the site of illicit encounters. Ilie had had a fight with his wife, who had left him and moved back in with her parents. Nothing prevented him from seeing Ileana now. Every Saturday, he would pick her up on the outskirts of Bucharest on the road to Alexandria. They would make love at least four or five times along the way. They would stop on the edge of the wheat fields or would sometimes rent a small room in one of the roadside motels. When the four of us were together in my yard, they would make obscene gestures at each other with their tongues, touch each other, and snuggle up to each other. Then, they would get up suddenly and go into the house or go back to Ilie's place. If they stayed at my house, they would use my grandparents' room, which I had moved out of, and would make sure we heard them going at it with their groans, moans, and even dirty talk.

Ileana had not spoken about her new lover, who was, in fact, my ex. She didn't feel at all guilty. Guilt was out of the question. She had always told me that love was a matter of competition. What could be more stupid than feeling hurt because Ilie no longer desired me?

"But, Ileana, my dear," I would have liked to say. "How could you make fun of my love, my longest-lasting love for a man?"

"Which man?" she might have asked. "This one? He's just a disposable object, like a condom."

"But we had got off to such a good start."

"Things like this always start well and end badly."

"But I had dreamed about getting together with him for so long."

"I can believe it, because you only care about the trivial things in life. You're made like that, you get worked up about nothing, about things that have little importance. Who else could you have loved, other than someone who doesn't deserve it?"

"So, nothing is worth rekindling?"

"Absolutely nothing, especially not something that is hurtful."

I would never have had the courage to launch into such a discussion unless Ileana had started it. We only used to talk about unimportant things, and even at that, we talked much less than before. My friend had realized that I was jealous, but she could also see that I found her relationship with Ilie funny.

Yes, it was true. Such goings-on amused me a lot, especially here, where they were of catastrophic importance, like the crash of a meteorite. No one could see us, no one understood our situation. However, it was impossible for our wrong to be righted. Our sins would be added to the big boulder of Guilt that had been launched by an avalanche, bringing our apocalyptic end ever closer. Betrayal, low self-esteem, and a lack of respect for others were as serious as incest, crime, mutilation, or torture. This coming and going from one partner to another was not at all normal: one day we would have to pay for failing to uphold the morality and decency of love. It was very clear that the people here had paid dearly. Ileana and I had become more obscene than monkeys. How were we going to be punished? How would our adventures end?

The purely physical relationship between Ileana and Ilie had created an even greater distance between me and George, my timid partner. Now that there was more space between us than just the size of a bedroom, I was deeply sorry about my behaviour the previous winter. I should not have suggested that we make love. Why wasn't I able to control my instincts before it was too late? How could I go back, how could I get myself out of this mess? If I had asked him to forget everything, if I had asked for forgiveness, would he have listened to me?

I was more and more conscious of George's age and found him less and less attractive. Because of his bad breath and pale, waxy skin, I would turn my back in bed. Yet, this position didn't in any way affect his sense of pride or hurt his feelings. He was born to withstand constant blows of this nature, like a fly without wings trapped in a jar. He was always at my side, he followed me like my shadow. He did not want to capitulate to Ilie and desperately tried to hang on to me. As soon as he saw his adversary, George would gently take my hand and hug me. He pleaded with me, meekly,

"Don't go to bed with him, I beg of you."

Despite George's vigilance, Ilie managed to slip me a note one day saying, "Back on Wednesday."

I was quite surprised. I couldn't believe that he was still thinking about me. Although Ileana was a more attractive woman than I was, it didn't matter very much to someone like him, who was used to changing partners often. For a long time, I didn't know whether to greet him like a real mistress, spruced up and elegant—heat and dust permitting, of course—or else to let things simply take their course. One thing was certain: I wasn't angry that he had cheated on me, or happy that he was coming back. As soon as Ilie stepped into my house, I would begin to kiss him passionately. A minute later, we would make our way to the bedroom, about to jump into the sack. Whenever he was at my side, I knew that Ilie would continue to be what he had always been to me: the eternal fiancé. As he would for the next thirty years. I didn't need to forgive him because he hadn't done anything to change our relationship, the spirit of which had floated through these spaces for years. If I erased Ilie from my life, what the hell would be left of my past?

In his presence, I once again used the power of gratitude, even for things of little consequence, as Ileana would say. I was grateful to Ilie for coming to see me, even for a few hours, and for making love to me, even though I sometimes felt that he was looking for Ileana through me.

After having sex, which I carried out to the very end, but only for my partner's pleasure, Ilie sat at the edge of the bed, with his back turned to me. He was smoking without paying much attention to me. It was as if I were not there.

That's why I loved him so much, actually. Because he came closest to my ideal hero. Even though he worked in a greenhouse, lived in a concrete block, and spent every day doing nothing but waking up, eating, going to work, and picking up women along the way, he was my hero. I admired him immensely for his primitive masculinity, for the indifference with which he would leave me and abandon me after having seduced me. He always behaved with the dignity of males who fertilize women without worrying about raising the little ones. After intercourse, he would just look for another herd, another harem of which he could become the master. Wasn't this how the world had developed? Without sentimentality or kindness.

We were both tired and calm, each of us with our own thoughts and sorrows. I then looked out the wide-open window and spotted Aunt Joana. Ilie seemed more frightened and offended than I by this unexpected turn of events. He did his best to get dressed quickly and avoid being caught naked by an old woman. I quickly pulled a dress over my bare-naked body, which had a strong smell of semen all over, without taking the time to wipe myself or even put panties on. I went out to greet my aunt like that. She hadn't been looking in the window, which was too high up for her, and she didn't look like she wanted to come into the house either. But Ilie had hidden in the last bedroom, a room I hadn't set foot in since the previous fall.

Aunt Joana had come to bring me a large round loaf of bread, a bag of sour cherries, the last ones of the season. She also handed me a slice of cake, wrapped in a linen napkin, which was as dry as dust. I was happy that she didn't want to come into the house, where pieces of mouldy bread, dried out cookies, and rancid cold cuts lay all over the place. My aunt also pulled out some candies, mixed with cookie crumbs, wrapped in a piece of newspaper. They were for Daniel. When I told her that he was gone, she put the candies in her pocket.

Aunt Joana began to question me all over again. Why didn't I ever visit her? How much longer was I going to stay here? Hadn't that damned womanizer, that rotten husband of mine, come to get me yet? As usual, it was always the other person's fault. I put on a depressed, even tragic, look, and answered,

"No, Auntie. He hasn't come yet."

She cursed him for a few minutes and then headed back home. As kind as she was, my aunt could not keep up a conversation with me indefinitely. Beyond the things that were absolutely necessary to talk about, apart from the trivial aspects of life or the weather, it was nearly impossible to find any topics of conversation. I walked her to the gate. I had just enough time to make a little noise warning Ilie to move away from the window.

The arrival of my aunt had put a damper on our pleasure. She had reminded us about things that both of us would have liked to forget. Ilie had already smoked a half pack of cigarettes and now he was attacking the other half with as much gusto. He asked me which of my father's sisters Joana was. Then he told me that her husband had tweaked his ears once, when he had tried to steal some pears.

We didn't have much time left. Ilie had to leave so he could be home again that evening and go to work the next day. We both felt that the minutes we had left were not enough for us to get close to one another again. The only answer was perhaps the bottle of vodka he had brought. Unfortunately, because he was driving back, he couldn't drink.

"No problem," I told him. "I'll drink alone."

He handed me the bottle, sat down on the edge of the bed, and watched me. I took a few sips and began to undress very confidently. Since coming here, I had done it so often that I had acquired the skill of a hooker. I had wanted to escape my husband's faithless love, as well as his body, which didn't interest me any longer. I thought I was moving toward a healthy form of asceticism after such a long period of uncertainty, but instead I had fallen into the trap of decadence.

I was still young and I didn't have many defects, other than slightly droopy breasts, a few stiff hairs around my nipples, and a few longer ones around my belly button and pubic area. I had a roll of fat around my waist, and a large mole under my left boob, but there was not much other body hair and I was not totally unsightly. No man would find me unattractive after seeing me completely naked, even without making love to me.

Ilie may have been crude person, like all rural folk, but he had the good sense not to let a woman offer herself for nothing, or to embarrass her by turning down her advances. Although he did not desire me, he accepted my invitation. The way he penetrated me, without much appetite to begin with, furious that he couldn't come as quickly as he would have liked to, convinced me of his immense masculine honesty.

I finally realized that I had been wrong about him. I had the wrong impression of my eternal fiancé. No, he couldn't make love with just anyone, any old time. He had not inherited all his father's faults, whereas I was just as naïve, just as simple, as my mother who couldn't stand up to the contempt of other people even though she understood it perfectly. In her boundless generosity, my mother forgave everyone easily.

From that moment on, I began to feel that my moral decline was not genetically induced. No one was to blame for my failures or the bad things that were happening to me. It was my fault, I was totally to blame.

I was the one who was making the mistakes, I was the one who was self-destructing. I was incapable of changing or improving my lot in life.

Ilie was not at all sorry to leave me. The instincts he had had as a fifteen-year-old were dead on and had not let him down. I was a girl with whom it was not worth having a relationship. I had nothing to attract a boy.

I screwed guys randomly and had no future. I was rigid, shy, without tenderness. Anything that went beyond the first contact was doomed to fail miserably, because I had all the qualities that were deadly for love.

I finally managed to cry, after having had so many chances to do so previously. These were neither the tears of salvation, nor the tears of relief. They were dry tears that intensified my despair.

How would the next thirty years of my life unfold?

August

The following month was even more depressing.

For me, it was one of those summers when the month of August was identical to the previous month. There was nothing to indicate the coming of autumn. The blistering heat continued to rage across the entire region and the torrid winds blowing from the South scorched the vegetation, drying out the fruit until they were shrivelled up and only the pits remained, enclosed in a wrinkled skin. The rains were a distant dream. In such a climate, the only thing that survived were the insects, which kept on breeding, and certain worms that fed on the sugar of the fruit, easily accessible now that the pulp had completely dried up. The only plus was that the heatwave had destroyed the mosquito nests that proliferated around the marshes, which were completely drained at this time of year. In the evening, I could stay outside as long as I wanted, dressed only in my old tank top and bare feet. The lice had also disappeared, in the absence of the animals that usually carried them. It was extremely rare to hear a dog barking at the other end of the village. You couldn't even tell whether cats were mating this year. When I was a girl, the rooftops would become veritable battlefields for tomcats.

Ileana and Ilie didn't come to the village anymore. They had left to spend their holidays on the beaches of the Black Sea. Because she was in love with Ilie, Ileana had ditched her poor actor, who had gone back to Chisinau after being thrown out of the apartment. She hadn't yet moved in with her new lover, however. If she hadn't, in my opinion, it was because Ilie hadn't asked her to. It would not have surprised me if he were discreetly preparing to break up with her. Ileana, for her part, had for some time been giving in to the advances of other men: a painter, a writer, a gynecologist, a bodyguard, a janitor, and a coroner. I could imagine the nightmare of spending her days on the beach with Ilie. Or perhaps she was enjoying pleasant evenings in little family restaurants with him. Ilie must have been missing everything: wild holiday nights, usually spent with his legendary groups of friends, heated arguments with rockers, mindless songs, random screwing behind a tree in a public park, and high-risk gambling with incredible sums of money lost in card games. Ileana now led this kind of life in the company of someone who knew a lot about football, who was quite well informed when it came to flowering plants, and who tended a vineyard that was half sterile. Sometimes, even Ileana needed to be punished.

In August, George moved in with me for good. He was now on holiday. He suggested that we go spend the summer somewhere, and perhaps join Ileana and Ilie at the little resort from which they were sending us post-cards. Or better still, we could go up into the mountains. He had saved enough money to pay for trips like this, with all the frills. George could afford to put us up for a few weeks in a comfortable hotel, with meals in clean restaurants that didn't have cockroaches. But I wasn't at all interested. I didn't want to leave my house. Perhaps that was the only reason I had come here, so that I would never again have to leave the village.

George took over all the chores in our newly formed household. He did all the housework: he cooked instant soups on an electric hotplate, he set and cleared the table, and he did the dishes. He was clean and tidy, but not showy in any way. George would have been able to tame any wild space, to make our life acceptable anywhere. He even knew how to do the laundry. In the evening, he would put the dirty clothes to soak in a basin of soapy water and the next day scrub them by hand. He was the one who now went shopping at the small grocery store run by our old classmate Dinut. In the summer months, farmers from neighbouring villages would display their produce on the ground against the side wall of the store: tomatoes, canary melons, watermelons, string beans, and pumpkins. They would pack up their carts in the evening and return the next day at dawn. The price of the vegetables they were selling remained as low as ever. George usually gave them twice their asking price. When we sat down at the table to eat our tomato salad, we would spend a lot of time talking about the disparity between the hard work of our parents and the paltry amount it was thought to be worth these days. We were sure that things would always be the same here. In any case, we would not be around to see any change. We would be dead before the lives of poor peasants improved.

George had attached new screens to the bedroom windows with thumbtacks. We could now open the windows day and night and keep the room fresh-smelling. George had also brought fresh sheets, which he washed every two weeks. He had placed a rug on the floor so that we could walk around barefoot indoors. We kept our sandals outside, reviving our parents' Oriental custom of taking their shoes off before entering the bedroom.

Everything connected to cooking and personal hygiene was moved to the veranda. George cleaned the cement floor thoroughly and repaired the cracks and holes. He set up an electric hot plate on a little table and put the dishes away in a cupboard. He kept a cover on the bucket of water to keep the dust off. He drove two nails into a pillar and hung towels on them. In the evening he filled the sink with clean water for getting washed in the morning. He had even brought a fridge which he filled with all kinds of food, including packets of noodles. That way we were able to get rid of the flies, ants, and cockroaches. The mice also disappeared from the house as soon as we threw out the carpets and woollen rugs. Only occasionally, at night, could we hear a rodent sharpening its teeth on the wooden rafters.

George continued to spend a lot of time at his mother's house, but that didn't bother me. He would repair her fence and roof; he would remove caterpillars from the trees and cut off the dead branches. That gave him an excuse for going to the centre of town every day. George was still keenly interested in newspapers, which he read with Dinut as they sat together on the wrought-iron bench in front of the store, where his mother and grandfather had once sat. George needed to keep up with what was going on in the outside world. He listened to the news on the radio, he tuned in to every broadcast, on every station, and then read about the same events later, in the papers, where they were described in the most minute detail. He lived in fear that, in his absence, changes might take place or important events occur: the government would be overthrown, there would be early elections, the dollar would again rise dramatically, the cost of rent, gas, bread, and shoes would go up. George was interested in everything outside his own life, in any drama fit to be commented on. But he couldn't get used to the fact that he had fragile teeth, broken bits of which would come off in pieces of bread, that he was prone to high blood pressure, that his hemorrhoids hurt, and that he had a hunched back. His mind was almost always turned outward. It would have been cruel punishment to make him take a closer look at himself, to force him to reflect on the future of our relationship, or to ask him to examine his true feelings about these things. And so, he put it off as long as possible.

He would look forward to spending beautiful summer evenings with Dinut at the store, after which they would sit for a few hours in a darkened bar room, drinking a cold beer together and bringing one back for me when he came home. He enjoyed riding his bike every day on the dusty roads that skirted the deserted houses. The people who had once lived in them were dead, but he hadn't known them. The only deaths that mattered to him were those of his mother and his grandfather. He was attached to them in his own way and looked up to them, although without much emotion. Besides, how could he be affected by things that hadn't been important to him in the first place? Why bother mourning for those he hadn't known even when they were alive?

Life with George was calm and convenient, with no questions asked. The only memories we shared willingly were of former teachers and the time spent in dark classrooms with low ceilings and a smell of oil, which had been spread on the floors to protect them from the damp.

Do you still remember how I would glance at you, nonchalantly, during anatomy classes, when they were teaching us about the fertilization of plants? When the teachers would talk about female reproductive organs, extracting square roots, the African continent, and hydrochloric acid? Do you still remember the smell of the coal-heated ceramic stoves, and the small puddles of water in which we cleaned off our boots before walking into the classroom? Do you remember how I walked you right up to the schoolyard gate in winter to protect you from snowballs? Or the time I took your red hat and gave it back to you two days later? Do you remember the teachers who didn't like you very much? And the times when you forgot to do your homework? How you couldn't wait for classes to be over? The day when you began to cry and told me that your mother had once again left your father?

Now that Ilie wasn't coming to see me anymore, George was less wary. Perhaps less in love too.

September

No, no, not his love.

Despite my indifference, the misery I surrounded myself with, and the other faults that he observed in silence, George continued to love me with all his heart. And while Marie and Zenaida feared, were indifferent to, or didn't understand the passion of men, I could not remain insensitive to it. George's love was so respectful and so tender that it moved me to tears. So much devotion could not end well. Only a catastrophe could put an end to my partner's passion.

In September, when his holidays were over, George suggested that I come to Craiova and live with him in his apartment. If I wanted to work, I could. Otherwise, no problem, I could stay at home. He knew how to make my life easy: without forcing me to work or slave away. After having experienced poverty for so long, George knew enough small tricks to make the life of a couple work. He had learned what was indispensable, and which other little things, trivial ones, we could dispense with to avoid spending a lot of money. We could live within our means comfortably and without making a lot of sacrifices. All I had to do was wait in the living room for him to come home. I could be happy every day, from morning to night, without lifting a finger. Unfortunately, George had attributed my unhappiness to the fact that I didn't want to work.

He didn't dare leave me alone again, in the midst of decay, after I had grown accustomed to a certain level of comfort once again. For the first time, George confessed that he didn't understand what I wanted or what I hoped to accomplish. How much longer was I going to stay here and why?

He had certainly forgotten the reason for my self-imposed exile. More and more, he convinced himself that there was actually no reason for it. I was the one who had made it all up, on principle, out of concern for my reputation. Mihai hadn't had a mistress, and I hadn't been fired. George was more and more convinced that it was all a lie.

He was probably right. I didn't know whether there was a real reason for my decision to come live here either. But how could I leave this place, how could I start my life over again, how could I go back to square one? With him or anyone else. Here or elsewhere. In Bucharest or in Craiova.

While George was talking about his plans for a peaceful and happy future, we heard a terrible noise, like the sudden breaking of a storm. Alarmed, we jumped out of our chairs under the apple tree, where we liked to take naps. We had to take cover. Was it an earthquake or was the sky falling in?

It was just a ceiling that had come crashing down, the one in the last bedroom, the guest room that looked out onto the street. The rafters had begun to cave in, bringing down a piece of the roof. The decaying walls, built with lattice beams, had also crumbled under the shock and had partially collapsed. This part of the house had imploded. A jumble of earth, bricks, and beams had fallen down with a terrible clatter, although without much dust. Luckily, between my room and the one that was in ruins, there was another room, only half of which had been affected.

My house now looked like an old, sinking ship, which was being dragged downward to the bottom of the sea. Or like a train, the last car of which had derailed. It was amazing how it had held up for so many years and suddenly could no longer resist the force of gravity, which was drawing it down to the depths of the earth. George tried to reassure me, explaining that it was because of the vibrations I had caused by opening and closing doors, and also because the rains had flooded the ground on which the house was built. Above all, it was my fault for having forgotten to repair the leaky roof I had told him about. If only I had replaced a few of the missing tiles or at least placed a few pots underneath the leaking spots to catch the water. But how could I remember my visit to the attic, last summer, at a time when I dreamed only of making love with Ilie?

Not long after this event and George's departure, my spirits lifted. I went over to the yard of the two old people who lived behind our house. The hemp ropes were still there, strung from one pillar to the next, from the front to the back of the property. I walked up two damaged steps and onto a cool patio, where I shaded my eyes with my hands and peered in through a dirty windowpane. In the middle of the bed, I saw just one body, hunched under the covers, but I couldn't tell which of the two old people it was. He or she was sleeping, their face turned toward the wall. I opened the door gently and walked into the room. Suddenly, quivering with fear, like a wild animal under attack from all sides, the one-armed man sat bolt upright in his bed. I stood planted on the threshold, looking at him. He had a blood-stained bandage wound around his blind eyes, and he reached out toward me, trying to grab or touch me.

"Is that you, Nikulina? It's you, tell me that it's you!"

Slowly, he tried to get out of bed, pulling the cover off to free his shod feet.

I rushed to the door without answering him. I could still hear him shouting for Nikulina until I reached the fence surrounding the property and exited through a gate made mainly of sunflower stalks.

Ilie came in the middle of September for the grape harvest, accompanied by his wife and brother-in-law, just like last year. Ileana was not around this time, and they didn't ask me to pitch in. After finishing her work and putting the must in the barrels, his wife came to my house bringing a basket of grapes and a bottle of grape juice. She was cheery and chattered incessantly about whatever popped into her head. She talked about her work, about the fact that she wanted to sell the old apartment to buy a bigger one, and about her hopes of maybe having a baby. She didn't say a word about her husband, or the fights they had. She didn't appear to blame me and didn't let on that she knew anything at all about our affair. She left again without inviting me for dinner at her house.

Oh! Something had to happen eventually, even in this place.

Once again, I could feel the onset of autumn. The impending season weighed on me all the time. I detected the imminent presence of nightmares in the yellow leaves that covered the yard and garden around me, the cold air that chilled the evenings, or the fog that cloaked the morning landscape. I would just be reliving the story of my grandfather, who had died of dysentery when no one took him to the hospital, according to my grandmother's wishes, the flood that had struck the village when I was three years old and during which I had spent two weeks sitting on sacks of wool on the roof with my mother, visions of cockroaches, crickets, and a string of apples tied to a ribbon, given to me when I lay hovering between life and death at the age of seven, Calin, the awkward and flatulent minstrel, my first period, the terrifying stories of girls who had been violently raped, which married women took pleasure in telling us, impossible childbirth, the cemetery from which villagers stole wooden crosses to burn in their stoves during harsh winters, the crazy woman on the street corner who hadn't cut or washed her hair for ten years, boiled milk, cheese strung up to let the whey drain.

I began to wander through the deserted village streets again. I was looking for adventure in places where there were only bad memories. I turned every corner of my own house upside down, as I did in the ruined houses around me. I was in search of something that would look unlike anything I had ever known.

The grape harvest had made the village come alive a bit. I saw more people around, but never familiar faces, never people I knew. I recognized the old familiar smell of sheep as soon as the fall mating period began. The strong, pungent odour of animal sperm permeated the air, even after the flocks of sheep and herds of goats had disappeared. The earth was infused with the hope that it would experience another green spring, full of flowers. Once again, I was overcome by memories of childhood, a childhood from which I could not escape, from which I could not free myself. Once again, I felt like I had been here forever.

I looked for Dinut in his cramped, dark store that smelled of diesel fuel. I wanted to talk to him, to reminisce about the hours we had spent at school, the way I had done with George. But the plump man just looked at me, curious but skittish. He responded briefly to cach of my comments and waited for me to leave as quickly as possible.

Once again, I began to search for adventure, for something to happen. Through the deserted orchard, the dry riverbed, the muddy pit into which garbage was dumped. Among the barren vines. At the edge of the cemetery where my parents were buried and where I hadn't even lit a candle next to the cross on their grave. In front of the statue of the unknown soldier. On the grounds of my little elementary school. Then my high school, where I had attended classes with my dear George, before I left for the lycée.

I never met anyone who wanted to get to know me and with whom I could have spoken.

Now, I went out even when it was raining. The cold no longer intimidated me. Thanks to George, I was now equipped with boots and a raincoat. If I felt I was catching a bit of a cold, I would go right back home to warm up next to the radiator and drink a piping hot coffee.

I continued to live in the large bedroom, which had become so familiar to me, and in which momentous events had taken place. I no longer felt threatened by the pile of rubble that lay outside my door. After a few desperate efforts, George had convinced me to move into my grandparents' shack, which was so small, so modest, but actually more robust. George left for Craiova, but only after helping me to get settled in with my bags and equipment. During his absence, however, I continued to sleep in the big bedroom from Monday to Friday, bringing only the radiator and coffee maker with me. Early on Saturday mornings, I would bring both machines back to the other building, where I would warm up the small room, make some coffee, and mess up the blankets in the middle of the bed so that it would look slept in.

George would arrive by car around noon. He had finally got used to travelling in his old Ford. Throughout the entire trip, he would cross his fingers that the car wouldn't leave him stranded in the middle of the fields. He had not yet exhausted the entire library. After going through the "Heritage," "Great Classics," "Philosophy," and "World Literature" collections, he was up to "Theology." A pile of massive tomes on the history of the Orthodox Church now lay on the armchair pulled up against the wall. Since last spring, there had also been a pile of art books from the "Meridian" collection, with pale and soiled reproductions but with the advantage of having large type. I asked George to leave them there for a while. They were actually the only books that I thumbed through occasionally. For the first time, I was trying to overcome my colour blindness. I had lived for an entire year the way I was the first day I arrived, relying exclusively on my sense of smell, the sense that was the seat of memory for me. I couldn't escape it. That's what had made me sick. Sick of memories. My entire life was concentrated in perfumes, odours, aromas, whiffs, scents, and stench. If I had been able to temper this sense somewhat, this cursed sense of smell, my stay here might have been more restorative and less devastating.

Most of the time, I turned to Cézanne. Some of his paintings helped me relive fragments of my past in a relatively bearable manner.

The painting *The Robbers and the Donkey* reminded me of the red riverbank at the edge of the village, where people made bricks out of clay. They would pour the clay into wooden moulds and then let it dry in the sun for several days. When I was little, I would go to the top of a small hill in the vineyards. In the distance, I would see donkeys waiting patiently to return to the stable, led by their masters. The tree drawn on the right side of the painting was the acacia in the shade of which the women would sit and eat at noon and rest a bit during periods of stifling heat.

The painting called *The Hermitage at Pontoise* reminded me of my great-grandfather Pantilie's big house, seen from the narrow path leading to the cemetery, where wild trees served as a natural border for the different properties.

Hanged Man's House touched me most. It showed just a small corner of Stela's house, where we counted from one to ten with our eyes closed when we played hide-and-seek. The faded colours were those of the summer sunset, when the women would gather around the well after finishing their work and talk for hours and hours.

Maincy Bridge depicted none other than our own bridge over the river, which we crossed in our carriages to take flour to the mill. We planted tobacco on the other side of the gentle slope that rose up from the river's edge. That's where a long thorn got stuck in my right heel, which I treated by soaking my foot for entire evenings in a pot filled with my own urine. We would also cross this bridge when my grandmother and I visited a godson who lived on Mill Road in the butchers' hamlet. My grandmother only rarely let me go with her because her godson's son was handicapped, and his saliva became mixed with mucus whenever he opened his mouth to eat or talk.

The Winding Road led right up to Aunt Joana's place, running through the hamlet where cheese was made. The third house was guarded by a big, brutal mastiff that would have torn passersby to shreds had it not been for a chain that kept it tied down. Beyond, the road climbed and wound its way around another house where a man lived alone, someone who had raped my mother in one of my nightmares. My mother told me that he had seduced a little girl, had gone to prison for it, and had never married because no one trusted him anymore.

At the time of this story, there was no one in the world who was more loved than my mother. I stuck to her like glue. She was young, beautiful, and so tender. My grandmother, my father's mother, was very hard on her, so much so that my mother would lose patience, pick me up in her arms, and leave the house to go back to her own parents. We would stay there for a few weeks until my father came to take us back home. My mother would cry while gathering up the remains of the meagre meals that my father ate alone, because he would refuse to eat with his parents, although he didn't hold it against them. He kept plates of bread and fish under his bed, which attracted ants. My mother made me laugh by running around with me on her back. When I left for school, she would watch me go for a long time. She never hit me, she didn't give me work to do, she didn't argue with me, and she didn't yell at me either. She never said no to me, and she believed all my lies. She didn't get angry with me when I didn't take the time to visit her in the last years of her life. My poor mother lost her life when she was crushed between two trucks loaded with corn.

The tree in *Large Pine and Red Earth* reminded me of the tall walnut tree on the northern edge of our vineyard, from which I could spot Ilie as he approached our property. During my summer break from the lycée, I would spend time with my friend Paula in the shade of its long branches under which no grass grew. We both wore glasses and read books we didn't understand at all. Toward sundown, my cousin Manole would arrive and tell us dirty stories. After nightfall, the shepherds would pass by as they returned from the pastures with their flocks. I waited to see Niculae, my bachelor cousin who lived behind our house. He was riding a small, sturdy, and stubborn donkey, which would sometimes break loose and devastate the neighbour's vegetable garden. After these antics, I would leave the house to avoid seeing the savage way the animal was beaten.

The Banks of the Marne reminded me of our large village church, seen from the yard of Aunt Flore, my father's elder sister, the one who had been adopted. On either side, people would dump refuse from their yards and manure, in which mushrooms and weeds would later thrive.

I closed the art book and curled up under the covers. I covered my head and tried as hard as I could to go to sleep.

The last days of September were so beautiful. It was hot and my childhood took on the sweet odour of burning leaves and sticky grape must, as thick as blood.

On a day like this, Zenaida would be landing on the shores of the terrible land of cheese. In the small port outside the city, warships returning victorious from the Trojan War were welcomed with flowers, cheers, tears, and banners. The people smelled bad, dressed poorly, and their skin was infected by mange and scabies, but they were the ones who had the good fortune to see their heroes again. Men gave jugs of wine to those who were just arriving. They hugged each other and kissed one another on the mouth, mouths that were full of rotten teeth, spreading the lice they had in their beards. Their sweat was even more acrid than that of the soldiers, whose odours had been dissipated by the wind and rain during their long Homeric adventure. But mothers and daughters had eyes for the slaves alone, for the half-naked prisoners. They were savagely jealous of the beautiful Cassandra and Zenaida. One of them was sitting cross-legged, pissing into her palms and spraying the urine on the submissive Asians who were threatening to undermine the peace and customs of their home.

Achilles had covered me with a purple cloak and hidden my face behind a veil, held on with a leather band. He held me with one hand while kissing his friends, uncles, cousins, aunts, and neighbours. He did not want my face to show. He told everyone that I was frightening, terribly ugly. He said that he had brought me back only because I was a kind of witch, because I knew a secret recipe for miraculous cures, because my hands could mend broken bones, and because I knew how to read the stars and the zodiac. People moved back respectfully when they met me. I could see only their bare feet, which were scaly, with long nails, and the muddy hem of their robes. At the same time, I looked at Achilles's heels and toes. He had washed them and cut his toenails before getting off the ship. His white tunic was very clean. Had he done all this for me? I had noticed something strange about him for a long time. His hair was no longer greasy and shiny, speckled with white dandruff. His beard was freshly combed, and his mustache didn't have traces of food in it.

What was I supposed to do? Bring the endless fight between Zenaida and Achille to a close? Get them to make up with each other? Could they live happily ever after, until they grew old?

October

In October, the rains began again.

I listened in silence to the rapid cadence of the raindrops as they tapped on the frame of my window, which had remained open throughout the summer. I hadn't yet removed the screens, although all the insects were now dead, having deposited their larvae in every tiny crack in the plaster, in the hidden holes of the garden, and under the bark of the trees.

Zenaida had also listened, for the first time, to the calm pitter-patter of the rain, gently muffled, like caravans gliding through the boundless desert. Through the open window of her room, the cool air was now seeping in, stroking and caressing her cheeks, sweeping in new and mysterious scents. Near her in their bed, made perhaps out of the wood of a single olive tree, Achilles lay in a deep sleep. He slept on his back and snored steadily. The scent of the wine he had drunk the night before lingered on his breath, and his shirt had the pungent smell of sweat generated after a day of working, riding, or archery practice. He hadn't yet acquired the habit of his brothers, who were all dead now, of undressing before going to bed and putting on a night shirt. Zenaida would teach him the customs of civilized life, discreetly. Gradually, almost unconsciously, Achilles would learn to wash his hands before meals and his feet before bedtime. He respected his wife when she had her period or when she was ovulating and did not touch her then.

Meanwhile, the Trojan princess took advantage of the Oriental custom of covering her face with a veil. She would wander through the fruit, vegetable, and fish markets, so unlike the opulent and abundant bazaars and souks of the Orient. She learned the Greek language easily, although she was astounded by the abundance of vulgar words and pithy expressions, by the perplexingly loose morals, and by the lack of hygiene during sex, as well as its frequency. The people here, even when they were exhausted after harsh labour in the marble quarries, on board fishing vessels, or on the Parthenon construction sites, were consumed by this single passion. In Athens, there were plenty of women who would accept indecent propositions from men, ranging from the highest aristocrat to the lowliest slave. Haughty *hetairai* would stroll through the crowded streets, using clay tablets to engrave the time of their assignations and the astronomical amount they charged, even negotiating the type of perverse activity and number of participants.

In this new country, the food was much greasier, saltier, and drier. There were no pilafs, tinted yellow with saffron, there were no spices to give sauces taste and colour, and there were none of the sweet and dry fruits of the oases. Here the oranges came from the hard and sterile soil of the Peloponnese peninsula and were stunted and bitter. In her own household, Zenaida had a hard time persuading the slaves not to cook with the water collected in the impluvium. The black slaves, who came from around the world, tried to point out that the water came from the sky and was therefore clean, but the princess insisted that they use it only for bathing and washing clothes. As the mistress of the house, she introduced Oriental hygiene in the kitchen, the bathrooms, bedrooms, rooftop terraces, and small garden in the inner courtyard. Every night, the large pots used for cooking meat were scrubbed and cleaned with sand until they were shiny. The kettles were no longer exposed to the flames of the fire but were protected with a stand that prevented them from becoming black. Bed linens and towels were changed once a week. The porcelain in the bathrooms was cleaned with ashes on the last Saturday of the month to remove traces of soap, restore the glimmering surfaces, and show off the alabaster mosaics depicting the sirens singing to Ulysses. Underpants were made for the women slaves to wear under their stiff skirts, so that there wouldn't be frizzy pubic hair left around, especially in the kitchen.

In this clean and organized household, which became increasingly aligned with foreign tastes, among people who respected her without having seen her face yet, Zenaida began to come to terms with her life. Every day, she would throw herself into her housework and daily routine, and dedicate herself to the inanimate objects over which she had some power. Priam's daughter ruled with wisdom over her domain of servants, beasts of burden, cats, and dogs. With each passing day, she persuaded herself that all of this was going to change her life.

Sometimes, at night, she would spend a long time gazing at the shimmering mirror of the sea. She always wondered what had happened to the courageous and wise Aeneas, the only one whose corpse she had not seen among the dead bodies piled up along the walls of Troy. It was said that only Aeneas had managed to flee the city in a ship full of warriors. Where was he travelling now? Which places were sheltering the last survivors of Troy, the last royal bone? Would they meet again one day to tell the world the tales of their earthly paradise?

Zenaida spent days and days grinding seeds and unknown grains in a wooden mill, preparing potions, ointments, and poultices for the fractured bones and wounds of paralytics, lepers, and the *hetairai* who got secret abortions after having relations with aristocrats. The people here were so naïve, so ignorant, that they would die even if they were in good health, from a mere cold, a burn, or a scratch. Zenaida brought them the blessing and the benefits of medicine, the kind of medicine that consisted in using the wild herbs that grew in the cracks of rocks, in distant corners of gardens, and transforming them into miraculous cures.

Achilles had allowed the rheumy-eyed, the lepers, the filthy, and the ulcerous to enter his house, where his wife would lay them down on a straw mat. She would drain their purulent sores, pour green, red or yellow potions on deep cuts, dig into their skin to pull out thorns or worms, and lance pustules. The beautiful princess would lift her veil for these people. She allowed the dying to see her face, more pure and more graceful than a morning at sea. She would nourish them with this last moment of beauty.

On days when it was quiet in her little infirmary, Zenaida taught female prisoners and slaves the secret of calming infusions. She showed them how to make dishes that were simple except for a single thread of saffron that could alter the colour and aroma. The mystery of taste lay in their mouths, on their smooth palates, or in the pink folds of their tongues, which could be rendered insensitive by a mere burn. These parts of the mouth had to be tricked or tantalized. Thanks to the sailors who sailed the seas across the world, Zenaida had access to all the particles, seeds, and kernels that could create this kind of illusion. She had to teach people that food could be seasoned not just with salt, but also with sugar, honey, bitter leaves, and lemon juice to which you could add miraculous pepper, vanilla, cinnamon, and ginger, a species known as "grains of paradise."

But what did the cold season, the harsh winter, really mean?

What do women and men do in this season, burrowed in their homes? They don't have parchment scrolls or manuscripts made of camel hide. There are no musicians or belly dancers. How could they stand the wet, white powder that fell from the heavens, covering the earth and turning it into a slippery mirror overnight? Why did the sun lose its power to keep plants green and vibrant in these parts?

The fire that burned in the hearth day and night brought everyone together. Men, women, and their livestock would gather around the fireplace, dressed in *touloupes*. With these sheepskin coats, they wore long woollen socks and fur hats. They looked more like scarecrows than people. These outfits concealed the beauty of women. You could no longer see their generous breasts, their round buttocks, their hips curved like the gentle hillsides, and their stunning legs. The skin on their cheeks and palms of their hands grew red and dry.

Oh, why had she placed so much hope in Aeneas? Why hadn't she thrown herself into the waves to die in the waters surrounding the magnificent city of Troy? How can you die, how can you kill yourself, here on this cursed ground? How could you let the priests scatter your ashes on the mud-covered shores instead of spreading them across the golden desert, during a sandstorm, the kind of storm that could have seeded the entire world with a tiny piece of your body? Zenaida had agreed to be taken to a land where you could neither live nor die.

The honking of a horn roused me from my dream. It was George's car. He had arrived. It had stopped raining two days earlier and the roads had dried up. The ground had been so thirsty after the summer's heat wave that it had swallowed up the cold drops of water with an insatiable appetite. George had brought a bagful of briquettes for the barbecue. He didn't want to use rotten wood anymore because it burned slowly and made the meat taste too smoky. He cooked two nice pieces of well-seasoned pork. We drank young wine that he had bought at a roadside stand from a producer. Then we watched TV while lying in bed. It was already cold in the bedroom. George's wife had packed up her things and finally left him. Unfortunately, he had run through the entire library. He had kept only one single collection, called "Our Mountains," which included guidebooks and tourist maps. He had deliberately saved these books for last so that we could look at them together and use them to plan our vacation.

Now I had to stop all my other voyages and allow my ship to finally dock in his port. We are going to get married, have children together, move to Craiova, redecorate our apartment, and keep Daniel with us. If I was ready, he would take me away from this place next week, for once and for all.

By pure chance, George had discovered that the little well in our yard still had water in it. After so many years of lying idle, the water table had been replenished, fed by underground streams as a result of the abundant rainfall. I drank the first cup of water from our well. The taste was not at all extraordinary. I remembered it perfectly, especially the sensation it left in my stomach. Everything that reminded me of my childhood seeped into my heart like sadness.

While George gathered the leaves in the yard with a long rake, I leaned over the mouth of the well and stared intently at the bottom. The depths were as dark as my soul.

Should I be happy about all that had happened, about everything that had taken place inside my decrepit fortress?

Enlightened by solitude, my mind had detected some fault lines in the solid concrete structure of my future. I had melted some narrow paths along this iceberg and reached some of the things that were awaiting me. And during these journeys, which had lasted but a fraction of a second, I had seen myself as I would be: fat, cantankerous, surly, angry, verbose, quarrelsome, and nagging. How awful! How much time would I waste drinking coffee? Reading tarot cards in a smaller and smaller circle of friends? My future would comprise fattening meals, with a lot of meat swimming in oil and sauce, gold jewellery, clothing made in China, hair dyed platinum blond. But my future didn't include a single book cover. I had had the respite and calm required to reach the collective unconscious, but I had missed the opportunity to derive what was essential from it. I had focussed only on a stupid love story. I hadn't retained anything else.

The ramshackle home I had come from was not just any old place. It was, in fact, a well, through which I could have descended to the depths of world history. If I had failed, it was due to circumstance, to chance, to the fact that I wasn't alone, that I didn't have the peace to relive everything from the beginning. During the first months of the previous winter, I had been one step away from a great discovery. But I had come back. It wasn't worth coming this far only to realize that my future as well as my past were so difficult to endure without an intermediary.

I woke up covered in dirt. The noise had probably stopped long since. I had been hit on the head by a beam. The crumbling clay around the wooden pillars had buried me alive. It was as if I had been entombed. I could no longer feel my body from my waist down to my feet. My hands were trapped, too. I had been imprisoned, lying on my left side. I felt that the falling tiles, bricks, and beams had crushed my shoulder and ribs. But were my heart, lungs, and kidneys intact?

I was not in agony. I felt no pain. I didn't know if I was bleeding. A shaft of light shone on me. I even thought that I could hear the rain pelting down. Yes, in the evening before going to sleep, I had heard the quick rhythm of the rain on the windowsill, as well as in the tub I had placed under the eaves. Then it must be dawn already.

But, my God, what day was it? Tuesday or Monday? Maybe it was already Wednesday. Really! And what if it was Thursday? I felt the dust in my mouth every time I opened it to take a breath of air. I was thirsty. I was crunching on the grains of sand that coated my tongue. There was a kind of thick glue bothering me on my left eyelid. The skin on my forehead was also dirty. I was beginning to feel many things again. I could even move my fingers!

When on earth had George left? Yesterday? I could remember walking up to the gate with him. Saturday! Don't forget. On Saturday, we are going to leave for good. I was warm. Heat was spreading throughout my body, from top to bottom.

I was once again travelling through the inside of the iceberg. I felt pain only if I tried to tear myself away from the silence of the ice.

Was I still asleep? Had I slept? I wrinkled my forehead. I blinked. My lips were clean now. I ran my tongue over my cracked lips, which were still bleeding.

Ah, yes. It was Friday. I was sure. Friday, without a doubt. I had gone to sleep in the evening thinking that I would have to move very quickly into my grandmother's bedroom at dawn the next morning.

Ah, I would be saved. Unfortunately, saved.

I stayed in the hospital for two months.

Mihai had found me lying there, almost buried under the debris. And yet, I had pulled through relatively well, with only a few broken ribs. I was as robust as my great-grandmother, Marie, who had been regularly beaten and her bones broken by Petre, according to my grandmother.

It was Wednesday. Mihai had come to see me. He wanted to persuade me, one last time, to stop being stubborn and leave the village. Half asleep, soaked in my own excrement, I could hear him calling me and shouting above the pile of rubble. He worked for several hours to dig me out. But I was out of danger. I could have survived for days and days longer because the roof, as it collapsed, had remained suspended half-way above my head, supported by the wooden trunk that stood next to my bed.

The doctors kept me under observation in the hospital for a long time, not because of my fractures, but because of the mental trauma brought about by the accident. I slept all the time, I didn't eat the meals they brought me, I refused to speak or didn't know how to speak. As well, although I appeared sane to them, I had experienced too much memory loss. I stayed in bed the entire day, in the same position as when they found me after the accident: lying on my left side, with my eyes closed, my palms clasped together and pressed against my cheek. I spoke to no one and did not answer questions either.

Gradually, I realized that Mihai, Daniel and Ileana were there, standing at the end of my bed every day. I recognized their voices and I remembered their names. But I didn't want to look at them.

Most of the time, I dreamed that I was on a raft floating on the ocean. The waves were rocking my body. Around me, there was a strong smell of feet and bleach. A piece of rancid cheese was hanging in a cloth bag near my nose. Achilles was putting a jug of water to my lips and I was drinking from it without opening my eyes. With a needle, he was digging into my skin looking for poison pills. No, I don't want to wake up. I will never leave this bed. If I do, he'll take me back to his cabin on board the ship and make me lie down on raw sheep hide. Again, I will have to put up with the smell of sweat. Again, I will have to use my fingers to clean up his disgusting yellowish semen, after he has filled the cavities of my body with it.

I don't know how much time I spent rocking gently on dark and murky seas before being carried in someone's arms and placed in another bed, in another room. They turned me onto my right side, so they could spread ointment on the bedsores on my left hip and armpit. I saw the white floor and a light fixture with only one working light bulb, which burned incessantly, even at night. A cobweb, which hung down so low I could almost touch it, vibrated at the slightest noise from the hallway.

The only one who dared to touch me was Daniel. They had shaved his head and there was an enormous bandage under his right eyebrow. His right hand was in a sling, tied to his neck with a red scarf. With the fingers of his left hand, he fiddled with my earring, just as he used to do when he was little, when I held him in my arms until he fell asleep. He asked me if I wanted to eat some bread.

Ileana made a point of coming at noon, once the nurse's aide was tired of trying to get me to eat. A tray with two plates remained on the table until Ileana arrived. By this time, the soup had congealed, the minced meat or stew was murky, and flies had started hovering over the piece of cake. For a good fifteen minutes, it would be Ileana's turn to try to pry open my closed lips so that she could get a few spoonsful of cold soup down.

One day, Ileana brought her new boyfriend to see me. I could see that he, too, was a redhead, with an imposing, freckled nose and a little tuft of hair growing under his lower lip. He was dressed in a sleeveless leather vest, which he wore with nothing underneath, showing off a large tattoo on his right shoulder with a black salamander breathing out red flames. The new lover was a swimmer. They had moved in together, in a place near the university, an old two-storey house built in an avant-garde architectural style. The rent was quite low because the building was falling down. A new earthquake wouldn't be needed for them to wake up one day buried alive under the debris. The landlords had left their apartments, preferring to rent them to students who didn't give a hoot about danger. In the evening, they held such wild parties that everyone feared for their windows. Ileana didn't care about privacy, which she had once adamantly demanded from her parents. In her apartment, nowadays, she would put up her partner's friends, who would come to the capital city at any time of the day or night, for some kind of championship, to go shopping, or just to party and get drunk.

Ileana told me these stories while her swimmer friend leaned up against the window and smoked. I understood everything. I could tell whether it was raining, whether the wind was blowing through the open window, or whether the cleaning lady was sweeping the hall. I knew whether it was the doctor who had come to see me, or whether his assistant was there instead to poke and prod at my hands and feet, for some reason.

Above all, I knew that Mihai's mother had died a few months earlier—he told me so—and that he had moved into her apartment, which was bigger and more elegant than ours, in the Camp Road neighbourhood. He had sold our apartment in Rahova. He asked me whether our friends could come to see me. When I shook my head to indicate no, it was the first conscious gesture I had made since coming back. He also told me that the company he worked for was looking to fill a vacant position for a secretary or translator—or both—and that we would be together all the time if I were hired. We would go to work and back in the car he had inherited from his parents. Always together.

I remembered the apartment my in-laws had lived in. It was on the second floor of a concrete apartment block, which was surrounded on all sides by other buildings of the same size and style, with square windows and enclosed balconies that were always full of laundry hanging up to dry. It was a quiet and clean neighbourhood, but without yards or gardens. No one would be planting onions there, no one would tend vines. You would never hear the rooster's piercing cry. The massive concrete structure would be a solid and very safe barrier against useless memories. Once again, the odours and seasons would lose their importance, their meaning, and their power. I would always have work to do. Having only one day off a week would not give me enough time to rummage through the past in search of ghosts.

What more could I do? At the age of thirty, I had taken a first and perhaps last step toward changing the course of my life. I had failed. Well, not entirely, perhaps. However, even though I had gained something, I wouldn't be able to take advantage of it. If I had learned something about myself, what was the point? I had suffered for nothing. I had finally realized that all efforts to combat decay are futile. I was no more talented at learning than your average person. All experiences left me cold. What's more, other people were going to force me to become really stupid. From now on, there would be nothing to stop me from falling.